ITALIAN ESCAPE WITH HER FAKE FIANCÉ

SOPHIE PEMBROKE

MILLS & BOON

First published in Great Britain 2020
by Mills & Boon, an imprint of HarperCollins*Publishers*
1 London Bridge Street, London, SE1 9GF

Large Print edition 2020

© 2020 Sophie Pembroke

ISBN: 978-0-263-08530-3

MIX
Paper from
responsible sources
FSC™ C007454

This book is produced from independently certified
FSC™ paper to ensure responsible forest management. For
more information visit www.harpercollins.co.uk/green.

Printed and bound in Great Britain
by CPI Group (UK) Ltd, Croydon, CR0 4YY

For my partners
in summer fairytale fiction,
Ally Blake and Cara Colter.

PROLOGUE

TALENT IS A funny old thing.

Some people have a talent for business, others a talent for mimicking accents or a talent for baking. Some have a talent for music—for creating it, playing it, sharing it with the world.

Like Daisy Mulligan.

I'm a music lover myself and, as head of the Ascot family fortune, have been able to indulge that love through events such as the Annual Ascot Music Festival and the new Ascot Music Awards. No one queries an old lady like myself meddling in modern music—they just assume I'm in it for financial reasons. Which is partially true, I suppose.

But money is something I've never been short of, and since I took over the family business I've only made more of it. And that financial security is something that gives me the ability to make the most of *my* talent.

I've never met another person with the same talent as me. I don't even know if one exists. It's certainly not something one talks about at the dinner table. Whenever I raised it with my mother I was told to be quiet, to stop being fanciful.

But at seventy-six, after almost a lifetime of study, I can confirm that my talent is, indeed, very real.

I know what people need.

Not what they *want*—which is a very different thing, and something they're far more likely to tell you up front, in my experience—but what they *need*.

And there's no way for me to shut that knowledge off.

As you can imagine, crowded places and large gatherings can be rather wearing, full of people subconsciously blasting me with their deepest needs. But this planet is full of people, so I've had to learn to cope with it.

And sometimes it gives me an opportunity to *do* something with my talent, too.

My talent and Daisy's talent collided at the Annual Ascot Music Festival in Copenhagen two years ago, when my beloved dog Max escaped. I twisted my ankle, and three lovely young ladies came to my rescue: Jessica, a Canadian, sat with me and fetched tea, while Daisy and Aubrey—British and Australian respectively—chased down Max and brought him home. Then the three girls took me to hospital and generally took care of me, making me laugh and keeping me entertained so that what could have been a terrible day turned into one of the best I'd enjoyed in a long time.

Three strangers, with far more important places to be and things to do, took time out from enjoying the festival to look after Max and me.

And I wanted to return the favour.

I kept track of them via social media, to be certain that my first read of their respective needs stayed constant. Then, when the time was right, I acted.

Jessica was first—a job offer in New York that, unplanned by myself, also led to romance.

Aubrey, poor dove, fell sick after we met, but now she's well again I know just what she needs too. Adventures are on the way for her!

But Daisy…

Daisy took a little more time to be sure. Since we met at the festival in Copenhagen her star has only risen. She's becoming a big name in her own right, touring the world and delighting fans with her music.

But that first feeling I had—the first need I sensed—has stayed constant.

She needs a home—something I suspect she hasn't had for a very long time. One that is entirely her own: her sanctuary, her refuge.

So I've given her the old house in Italy. I suspect it'll need some work, but that's intentional. After all, how much value do we place on things we don't have to work for? Making that house a home will be her responsibility and, knowing Daisy, she'll appreciate it far more believing that she's earned it. In fact, if I gave her, say, a pristine villa in Spain, she'd probably run a mile.

This house will take love and effort and care.

But I know that it will repay her.

A home, after all, is one of the greatest treasures we possess. Well, a home and someone to share it with, perhaps. But love is firmly outside my remit *and* my experience.

I have my doggie companions, and they are home enough for me.

But I confess I'm intrigued to see what Daisy will make of her new home…

CHAPTER ONE

JAY BARWELL LOOKED out into the stadium, squinting against the lights to try and make out even the front row of the audience. He was losing them. He could tell that much, even if he couldn't see them.

All those adoring fans who'd trailed around after him whenever he was out in LA or London or Dallas with Milli. Those loyal followers who'd been listening to Dept 135's music practically since he and his brother Harry formed the band. The casual listeners who heard them on the radio and found themselves humming along, who'd come to a gig to see if they were as good live.

He was losing all of them.

The band could feel it too, he knew. Harry's guitar riffs sounded tense, somehow, and Nico's beat on the drums wasn't as crisp as it should be. Even Benji's bass guitar was just off, somehow. And Jay knew it was all his fault. He was off his game, had been ever since Milli walked out on him.

He needed to pull it together. He needed to put on a show—one worthy of the ticket price these people had paid to see them play.

Jay just wished he knew how.

He was too far inside his own head, that was the problem. Too caught up in his own failings to be good at anything. Maybe Harry had been right, maybe going out on such a long tour so soon after the breakup was a bad idea. But Jay had been sure it was what he needed—a distraction from the rest of his life falling apart. From the discovery that all the things he'd thought he had were fake all along.

The song wound to a close, going out with a whimper rather than a bang. There was applause, of course, but it felt more polite than genuine.

Jay turned to the side of the stage and saw Daisy Mulligan, their support act, watching with a frown, her bottom lip caught between her teeth. She was young, new on the circuit, technically still star struck by them all—and yet even she could obviously tell something was off tonight.

If it had been one bad gig, Jay might have written it off—every band had an off night now and then, right? But this whole tour seemed to be one bad gig after another, and he just didn't know how to fix it.

At least the next item on the set list was a duet. He and the guys had met Daisy at a festival in Copenhagen a couple of years before, where she'd ended up onstage with them singing one of their bigger hits, 'With You', adding harmonies and a whole new level of meaning to the simple love song. When she'd agreed to come on tour with them as their support act, Jay had suggested they add the duet into the set list. Which was just as well, since night after night it seemed to be the only song that got a genuine response from the crowd.

Picking up her trademark mandolin, Daisy crossed the stage to join him.

'You okay?' she murmured as they took their positions, her words masked by the cheers from the auditorium. They'd already heard Daisy play once tonight and, unlike Dept 135, Jay had to admit that the young singer-songwriter was having a stellar tour. At least the label would be pleased about that much, he supposed. As long as she could continue to keep her notorious firecracker temper in check.

'Fine.' He shook his head. 'Let's do this.'

The difference was obvious the moment the music started. With Daisy onstage beside him, he could focus on her rather than the crowd. He felt the chords vibrate through him, thc high counterpoint Daisy played on her mandolin cutting through their more usual riffs.

She caught his eye as they both took a breath, ready for the first words, and for the first time since they'd last sung together the night before, Jay felt centred. Ready. As if he was where he needed to be.

These days, he seemed to be living for these few minutes when he managed to lose himself in the music again, in a way that had been eluding him ever since Milli left. Since he'd realised that what he'd thought was true love was actually all just another performance.

The crowd could obviously feel it too; a hush fell over them as Jay and Daisy sang, the harmonies rising and soaring above their heads. Jay felt the tension start to leave his shoulders. Hopefully they could finish this gig on a high, if he could keep this energy going into their finale number, next.

Maybe he wasn't completely washed up at thirty.

He'd leaned in closer as they sang, he realised, and so had Daisy. There was so much emotion in the words, in the music, that it felt natural. They were singing a love song, after all.

She smiled up at him, her eyes dancing, and he realised—not exactly for the first time—that she was gorgeous. Big green eyes under dark hair, her petite form meaning she barely came up to his shoulder.

Perhaps it was that revelation, or perhaps

just the relief that the crowd were back on side, that this song at least sounded good. Whatever the reason, as the last notes faded away Jay wrapped an arm around Daisy's waist and held her close, while the crowd cheered in a way they hadn't since he'd stepped onto the stage.

He leant closer, meaning to murmur his thanks to her. But then he got caught in those eyes, in the cheers, in the atmosphere. And before he even knew what he was doing, Jay pressed his mouth to Daisy's—the brief kiss sending the audience into ecstatic cheers, and his body into the sort of reaction he hadn't felt in months.

It was only as he pulled away and watched the dazed look fade from Daisy's eyes, instantly replaced with a more familiar flashing anger, that he realised how much trouble he was going to be in when he got offstage.

The sound of the crowd still rang in Daisy's ears as she stepped off the stage two nights later—and into her own personal hell.

'Daisy! That was a great gig. You must be

so pleased. Do you think you and Jay will celebrate together later? Will you join him back onstage for an encore? Off the record, can you confirm *anything* about your relationship?'

No. Because there is no relationship.

She could tell the damn reporter that, but Daisy knew from experience she wouldn't believe her. And why would she, after that bloody kiss Jay had planted on her after their duet in Philadelphia, two days ago?

He'd apologised afterwards, of course, muttering something about trying to put on a show for the crowd—and Kevin, their manager, had been thrilled. Photos of the kiss had been all over the Internet in a matter of hours, and sales for the remaining nights of their tour had seen a sudden surge with all the speculation about their supposed relationship.

The truth, it seemed, didn't matter so much in situations like this. Another thing to learn about being an almost celebrity.

Daisy knew it was all just an act. But knowing that didn't stop the buzz of connection that had hummed through her like a melody when Jay had kissed her...

The reporter was still waiting for an answer. Daisy yanked her thoughts back to reality and belatedly found some words for her.

'Yeah, it went well. Great crowd out there tonight.'

That much, at least, was true. Unlike all the rumours about her and Jay.

There were more questions—there were always more questions, and too many reporters asking them. Daisy had never imagined anybody being quite so interested in her life offstage. Hell, she'd never imagined them being that interested in her music *on*-stage. But ever since that festival in Copenhagen, life had generally been beyond her wildest expectations and dreams.

Copenhagen had given her more than her career though. It'd given her friends too. Not just Jay, and the rest of his band—Dept 135—but also it was where she had met her two best friends in the world. Two women she'd spent mere hours with in person, on that one day at the festival when they'd helped an old lady, Viv, and her dog, and ended up hanging out the rest of the night.

They might not have seen each other since that day in Denmark, but they'd stayed in touch. In fact, Jessica and Aubrey had been a lifeline for Daisy in the months that followed, as her whole world turned upside down when fame came calling.

They'd had their own issues too. Aubrey had been seriously ill, although finally seemed on the mend, and ready to take on life on her own terms again. Jessica, meanwhile, had just been offered an exciting job opportunity in New York.

While Daisy had everything she'd ever dreamt of. She was performing nightly on a world tour, singing her own songs, playing her own instruments, supporting one of the biggest bands in the world. And if you believed the media, she was also involved in a wild romance with Jay Barwell, voted world's sexiest man three years running.

Of course, that part was total fiction, one that had been doing the rounds even *before* the infamous kiss. Daisy happened to know that Jay was still totally hung up on his ex-girlfriend—American popstress Milli Masters. She suspected that was the real reason he'd kissed her—to show Milli he was over her, even if he wasn't. Daisy could understand that, and could live with the rumours to a point—after all, she owed Jay a lot.

Just not enough to have to deal with the paparazzi quizzing her about her sex life every night after a gig.

Forcing herself to smile, she pushed through the crowd—stopping to sign a few autographs for fans at the edge of the throng—ignoring more shouted questions about her imaginary love life.

'Daisy! Is it true Jay took you to Paris for your birthday?'

'Do you think he's going to propose soon?'

Oh, how disappointed they'd all be if they knew that Daisy had spent her birthday alone in her hotel room, apart from a video call with Aubrey and Jessica during which they sang 'Happy Birthday' to her.

She hadn't even told Jay or the guys that it *was* her birthday. It was a rare night off in the tour schedule, after a day of travelling to the next location, and all she'd wanted to do was sleep. That was all she ever seemed to have the energy to do between gigs, these days. The glamour of the celebrity lifestyle had *definitely* been exaggerated in her case.

As for proposing. Ha! Even if they *were* dating, Daisy knew that wouldn't happen.

She wasn't the settling-down type. Staying in one place too long had never been her scene. In fact, she'd spent the first sixteen years of her life fighting to get *out* of the place she'd been born and brought up. There was too much world to see, too much life to live, to settle down and stay with just one person.

Her home was on the road, her people were the musicians she met there and her true friends scattered across the world— Aubrey in Australia and Jessica in Canada, or New York, now. The only things she held sacred were her guitar, her mandolin, and her own voice.

What else did she need, really? Except perhaps a decent night's sleep somewhere that wasn't a bus, and the space to clear her head for a few minutes without someone asking her something or calling her name.

'Daisy Louise Mulligan?'

Somehow, through the clamour of the crowd, the music still raging through the speakers around the stadium, and the questions she was trying to ignore, Daisy heard her full name—spoken softly, but insistently.

Frowning, she turned to try and figure out who'd spoken it. Her eye fell upon a nondescript man in a grey suit. Not a pushy paparazzi for sure, and definitely not one of her typical fans.

'Yes?'

'If you could come with me, please, I have some important legal information to share with you.'

Daisy shrank back. Oh, she didn't like the sound of that. In her life 'legal information' usually meant a lot of trouble. Except she was pretty sure she hadn't done anything even vaguely illegal since she left home at sixteen.

Maybe she was being sued. That was the sort of thing that happened once you started to get famous, right? Jay had definitely been sued before—although the case was thrown out of court because of course he hadn't done anything wrong. Jay was a sweetheart. That was why the whole world loved him so much.

Of course, the rest of the world didn't have to see him moping around about Milli bloody Masters, or deal with his grumpy moods since they split up six months ago. That probably helped.

But back to the problem at hand.

'Am I being sued?' she asked.

The man in the suit gave her a faint smile and shook his head. 'Quite the opposite, Miss Mulligan. In fact, I have some very good news for you.'

Daisy drew back a little more. Somehow, the idea of *good* news made her even more nervous. She was used to bad news, to disaster, to problems. And she figured she'd already used up all the good luck she was entitled to in her whole life by getting the gig as the opening act for Jay and the band.

Whatever this news was, Daisy was certain there'd be a catch. Good things didn't just *happen* to people. Daisy knew that there was always a price to pay somewhere. If her childhood had taught her anything it was that she had to work for anything good that came her way—she couldn't just rely on hope and the kindness of strangers.

'If you could just come with me?' The man held out his arm for Daisy to take.

Her eyes widened even further, and she took a step back.

He dropped his arm, seeming to get her measure. 'There's a coffee shop, just across the way. Brightly lit, plenty of people. If you will join me there, I'll be able to fill you in on all the details of your inheritance.'

Daisy looked across the road and saw the coffee shop he'd mentioned. It looked safe. And not full of reporters asking her questions.

Then her brain caught up with his other words.

'My inheritance?' She didn't have anybody who owned anything to leave her, as far as she knew. Her own family had barely had enough money to buy food for the many kids crammed into their council house. 'Someone left me something? Who?'

But the man in the suit didn't answer the question she asked. Instead, he answered a different one.

'Yes. You've been left a house—well, a cottage. A villa, perhaps? In Italy. Now, if you'll come with me...'

She followed him in a daze. A cottage? Why would *anybody* leave her a cottage, in Italy of all places? A cottage sounded like... well, like a *home*. And she hadn't had one of those since she'd run away from Liverpool at sixteen with her mother's old mandolin and a change of clothes, and barely looked back.

This had to be a mistake. She'd go with the guy, figure out what confusion had sent him here, to her, and then she'd get back to her regularly scheduled life. Her manic, overloaded, exhausting life, full of fake news about her romantic status.

Great.

Another day, another lousy gig. The duet with Daisy had been the only bright point, yet again—although he'd managed to keep his lips off her for the last couple of nights, so even that hadn't gone down as well as it had in Philadelphia.

Jay handed his precious guitar to the stagehand, waved wearily at the rest the band—ignoring a concerned look from his brother, Harry—and headed for the stage door. He should go back to the dressing room, he knew. Get changed, freshen up, hang with the band, listen to their manager, Kevin, tell them what a great job they did tonight. But to be honest? He couldn't face it.

Daisy had come back out for an encore with them, at the end of their set, which he hoped meant she'd forgiven him for the kiss—but might just mean she was trying to save him from himself. She was good, Jay had to admit. From the first time he'd seen her play in Copenhagen, two years ago now, he'd known her talent was something rare and special. It was a point of professional pride that he had brought her on board, although it helped that her music and style, while complementing theirs, was different enough from Dept 135's offerings that they were never in direct competition.

She got on well enough with the rest of the band too—and Jay knew from previous experience that wasn't always the case with supporting acts. Overall, it had been a good decision to ask her to open for them on this tour. But Jay had a feeling it was starting to get to her.

The touring lifestyle wasn't for everybody. Hell, he wasn't even sure it was for him, and he'd been doing it for the better part of a decade now. But it was what you had to do to make it in the music industry these days. And Daisy was great onstage, always had been. The problems only started offstage.

Jay knew that in his current state of mind, he probably wasn't the best choice to be lecturing anybody about positive attitude, or the benefits of not snapping at the management—especially since it was his lips that had increased the pressure on her from the paparazzi. Still, he couldn't help but feel that, as her mentor of sorts, it was his place to have a word with her before she really hacked someone off. Even Harry, the most even-tempered guy Jay knew, had raised his eyebrows when Daisy had stormed off straight after sound check, leaving her precious mandolin behind for someone else to store safely until the gig that night.

When they'd first met, Daisy had hugged that mandolin like a safety blanket. Jay couldn't help but think that this afternoon's mini strop signalled worse things to come, and it was his job as band frontman, and Daisy's sort-of mentor, to try and nip that in the bud.

Leaving the others to head back to the dressing room for a well-deserved drink and pat on the back from the management,

Jay followed Daisy's retreating figure out through the stage door instead. She had a head start on him, but he could just about see her mop of dark hair bobbing through the crowd of journos and fans. She stopped to sign some autographs, which was a good sign. When she stopped making time for the people who listened to her music, then she'd be in real trouble.

'Jay!' Pamela Pearson, one of Jay's least favourite music journalists—if he could call someone who only ever reported on the personal lives of musicians, rather than the music they made, that—elbowed her way to the front of the crowd at the stage door to grab his arm. 'It's so good to see you again! And looking so happy, too. Are we to assume that's since you brought Daisy on tour with you this time…?'

She didn't actually wink, but she might as well have done.

Last year, when they'd toured, Daisy hadn't been enough of a name to join them as an opening act, and they'd already had a commitment with another band for the slot, anyway. But ever since Jay had introduced Daisy to their manager, dragging Kevin to see her play in some dive bar in London, after he recognised her name from that festival in Copenhagen, their musical stars had been somewhat linked.

Phoenix Records, their label, had a great reputation for nurturing new talent, and part of that was pairing new artists with established stars to help them through the growing pains that every musician went through, trying to adapt from playing music for themselves and twenty people in a pub to making music for millions. Jay had been an obvious choice to mentor Daisy, so they'd stayed in touch through the year.

Then, it had been low-key enough that no one outside the band or the label had even noticed. Well, apart from Milli, but Jay wasn't thinking about her. Ever again.

Although, it had been his break-up with Milli that had made him so adamant he wanted to get back out on the road, and quickly. He'd assured Kevin and the label that they'd be able to work on the new album while touring, which everyone had to know was a lie, but they'd let him get away with it anyway. Perhaps they knew as well as he did that staying at home, noticing all the places Milli wasn't, wouldn't help him at all.

Heartbreak was supposed to be good for inspiration, but so far Jay hadn't found any music in his misery. At least, nothing that was repeatable to the world at large.

Bringing Daisy on tour had suddenly brought her to the notice of music journos— and gossip reporters—everywhere. And given that Jay was her main friend, supporter and mentor on this tour, people had begun jumping to the usual boring and predictable conclusions. Helped out by that accidental kiss in Philadelphia.

They were wrong, of course, but it did serve as a nice distraction from the endless articles about how he was moping over Milli, while she was off holidaying with some billionaire businessman in the Maldives.

Not that he read those articles. Much.

Mostly because Harry confiscated them.

'Pamela, I'm always happy after a great gig like tonight.' He flashed the reporter a blinding smile, just one more person in the industry he was obligated to charm. 'And having Daisy on tour with us is just an added bonus. She's fantastic fun, on-stage and off.'

Dammit. Jay regretted the words the moment they were out of his mouth and cursed himself doubly when he saw the shark-like grin that spread across Pamela's face. She was going to take that as further confirmation of their relationship and run with it, Jay knew. And since the Daisy being fun off-stage part was currently a total lie, he knew he'd pay for it once it reached her ears.

'I must say, as a friend, it's just so lovely to see you happy again, Jay.' Pamela laid a hand on his arm, and he resisted the urge to shake it off. They weren't friends, they were barely acquaintances. But that wouldn't stop Pamela butting into his private life. 'Might we keep hoping for an official announcement soon? Maybe even a shot of Daisy flashing some extra-special jewellery?'

In for a penny, in for a pound, as his gran always used to say. If Pamela was going to write about him and Daisy anyway, it might as well be a story that would show Milli he really had moved on from her and her betrayal. One that didn't talk about how tired he looked, how downhearted, how he'd lost his way and his music was suffering. He was so sick of *those* articles.

'Never give up hope, Pamela. That's what I always say.' And with a wink, Jay headed out into the crowd to find his wayward support act, hoping she wouldn't actually injure him when she discovered he was fuelling the rumours about their romantic lives.

CHAPTER TWO

'WHERE WERE YOU last night?'

Daisy closed the hard guitar case with her instrument inside and fastened the clasps. Her guitar wasn't quite as precious to her as her mandolin, but it was still one of the tools of her trade, and that meant she needed to take good care of it. Something she had to remind herself to do when frustration and anger got the better of her, and all she wanted to do was be alone away from idiots. At least musical instruments didn't ask annoying questions. Unlike Jay.

She turned to him with a sigh. 'I was onstage with you, same as every night. In fact, I was carrying the whole damn gig, just like *every* night of this tour. And then I was sleeping on a tour bus to get here. Also the same as you. Except I wasn't snoring.'

'I don't snore. That's Harry.' Jay hopped up to sit onstage beside where she was packing up her equipment after the sound check, close enough that she had to move around him as she worked. One thing she'd learned about Jay while they'd been touring—he had no sense of personal space. Which meant they all got to share his miserable mood. 'And I meant between those two things. Where did you go after the gig? You left me to deal with Pamela the shark all on my own.' He nudged her leg as she passed, obviously hoping to raise a smile with his use of the nickname. He was making an effort, more than he did most days. She supposed she should be pleased by that.

In fact, though, he just reminded her exactly why she was annoyed with him.

'I thought you and Pammy were big mates,' Daisy said. 'At least that's what she's claiming on her blog this morning, as she spills all the details of your private friendly chat about your relationship with me. I understand I should be anticipating some diamonds soon.'

As if. Daisy had always known she wasn't the marrying kind—not even the settling-down sort. Even if Jay was interested in her—which, since she knew he was totally hung up on his ex, Milli, he categorically wasn't, that surprisingly intense kiss not-withstanding—all these stories presupposed that she'd just fall at his feet. Because to the world at large, Jay Barwell was the dream, the fantasy, and no one in their right mind would turn down the opportunity to bed him, let alone marry him.

Well, apart from Milli Masters, who was her own fantasy fodder to millions—even more so than Jay.

And Daisy. Who had absolutely no interest in marrying anyone, especially not a guy who snored on tour buses and tried to 'big brother' her. He called it 'mentoring' but Daisy knew what it *really* was. It was Jay thinking he knew better than her about everything, and that had never gone down well with her.

Especially since *his* attempts at managing the press now had her practically engaged to him. So much for knowing best. *She'd* never got them accidentally engaged before. Although that might be because she avoided media—social and real world—as much as possible. Something else Jay thought she was wrong about.

Jay laughed. 'You know Pamela. Never one to bother with the truth, when the lie is so much more interesting.'

'Interesting,' Daisy muttered. 'That's one word for it.'

Daisy didn't understand that—or how he could be so blasé about it all. She could sort of get going along with the rumours and the gossip—even her limited PR knowledge told her that people talking about them, whatever the reason, had to be good publicity for the music. Which was, in case the whole crazy world had forgotten, what they were actually there for.

But when it came to outright lies about them, to pretending they were madly in love and getting married…well, that was where she started to get twitchy about the whole thing. Not least because it was completely unbelievable.

She tried to imagine her family, such as it was, back in Liverpool reading these headlines: *Rising star Daisy Mulligan set to tie the knot with superstar Jay Barwell!*

Yeah—no. She could see her gran laughing now, so hard she'd give herself another coughing fit. And her dad would just roll his eyes and toss the paper out. Her little brothers probably wouldn't even remember her well enough to comment, and her stepmum would use the paper to pick up the mess the dogs left in the back garden.

Her life didn't come with fairy-tale weddings and happy ever afters, even fake ones. Of course, it hadn't come with Italian villas until last night, either.

'You didn't answer my question.' Jay leant closer, right up into her space, and Daisy forced herself to stay still to avoid giving him the satisfaction of backing away. She tried to ignore the way her body hummed with the memory of that fake kiss, too. That wasn't going to be any help at all in this situation. 'Where did you go after the gig last night? I came looking for you.'

She didn't ask why he'd been looking in the first place, because she could guess— and it had nothing to do with getting on one knee with a diamond ring, or even kissing her for real this time. He'd probably wanted to talk to her about her attitude. Again.

As if her basic personality was something she could just change to suit him. Uh…no, thanks.

'Some guy came looking for me. A lawyer, I guess. Wanted to talk to me about an inheritance.'

Jay's sandy eyebrows went up at that. 'Someone died?'

Daisy frowned. The solicitor hadn't explained that part. Usually when you inherited something, someone had to die first, right? But in this case it seemed more like a mystery gift. And it wasn't as if she had any rich relatives to die and leave her stuff, anyway. When her gran went, she'd be lucky to inherit her old Zippo lighter, at a push.

'I'm not sure. It was kind of confusing. But basically, someone seems to have left me some cottage in Italy, for some reason. It's probably some sort of scam, I don't know.'

None of it made any sense at all, and from the baffled look on Jay's face, he knew it. And she'd never even told him about her family, or how she'd left them behind at sixteen and never looked back. Maybe he'd guessed some of it, but she'd never *told* him.

She never told anybody. The past was just that—past. Daisy had no intention of living in it.

But if Jay had questions, he didn't have the chance to ask them, because at that moment Kevin, their shared manager, came bustling into the auditorium, his eyes fixed as ever on the tablet in his hands.

'Guys! Have you seen this? This is immense. The organic reach of this story has been incredible. Ever since that kiss! We *have* to capitalise on this, stat.'

Daisy and Jay exchanged wary glances. Kevin wasn't naturally an over-excitable sort.

'Seen what, exactly?' Jay asked. Daisy was happy to leave whatever this was to him to resolve. After all, he was the senior artist on the roster, the headlining act. She was just support.

Plus he was much less likely to snap sarcastically at Kevin than she was. Daisy knew her limits and, after three months of constant touring, she was pretty near them. She needed her own space—something that was non-existent on tour. Plus the mental strain of keeping everything together when all the reviews talked about how Dept 135 weren't living up to their reputation, how her duet with Jay was the best bit about the show... She was glad people liked what she was doing, of course, but it didn't make for a great feeling on the bus, and she knew it was getting to Jay. She needed some time away from them all.

Thank God tomorrow night was their last show before a three-week break. Three weeks on her own, without having to make small talk or be polite to people or pretend she cared about marketing strategies and branding…that would be perfect. She could recharge—alone, probably in a hotel room somewhere with great bars nearby, and an anonymous city vibe—and come back to the tour ready to be polite to people again.

Well, as polite as she ever got, anyway.

Kevin turned the tablet towards them, showcasing a shot of the two of them on-stage in Philadelphia, the moment that they kissed. The headline above it read: *Wedding Bells for Jay?* Daisy pulled a face and started to turn away—until Kevin flipped to the next photo, one that must have been taken just moments later, after the kiss but before she walked offstage.

She couldn't help herself. Daisy leaned closer and studied the picture.

No wonder people were believing these crazy rumours. They looked like they were in love. No doubt about it, the connection between them onstage was clear for anyone who even glimpsed the photo.

She stared at the screen, fascinated. She'd known, ever since that festival in Copenhagen where they'd first played together, that they had a musical synchronicity. Without ever rehearsing or even playing together before, they'd been able to just sink into each other's style and *play*. When Jay played guitar she could just *feel* where he was going from chord to chord and, with her mandolin in her hand, she could dance around the tune he summoned and add sparkle and chimes and an extra layer of magic.

Of course, they were still much better when they actually practised, but that didn't change what lay under the music, or what she saw in the photo Kevin was proudly displaying.

When she and Jay made music together, she knew him, understood him, in a way she didn't understand *anyone* outside music. Which probably had more to do with her lack of social skills than anything else, but still. When they played, they connected.

And that showed, even in a photo, even

without the kiss, even without the music there to explain it.

But without the music that connection didn't make any sense. Unless the two people in that photo were in love.

'That's so misleading,' she said sharply, forgetting her resolve to let Jay deal with this. 'They're reading too much into a fake kiss that only happened because Jay knew the band were tanking that night.'

Jay winced at that, but didn't argue back, which Daisy figured made her case for her.

'Is it?' Kevin raised his eyebrows. 'I mean, it happened—happens every night you play together onstage, whether you kiss or not. And if your fans read a little more into it than is technically true...that's not our fault. It's our opportunity.'

Rubbing his hand across his forehead, Jay sank back down to sit on the edge of the stage. 'This is because I spoke to Pamela last night, isn't it?'

Kevin scrolled up the screen on his tablet to show another headline on the gossip site: *Jay says he's ready to love again!*

Daisy snorted as Jay said, 'I didn't say that!'

'Doesn't matter what you said.' Kevin put the tablet down, for possibly the first time since Daisy had met him. She suspected he even held onto it in his sleep. 'What matters is what the world believes. And they believe—no, they *know*—that the two of you are in love. And that gives us an opportunity.'

'To do what, exactly?' Daisy asked, instantly suspicious. She had a feeling that whatever it was it would have nothing to do with music—which was all she was interested in. And she was starting to suspect that this had nothing to do with what *she* wanted at all.

'To raise your stars further! To give your audience what they really want!' Kevin's voice vibrated with excitement. 'And to make a lot of money, I hope,' he added, more prosaically.

It always came down to money, Daisy knew. And having lived so long without any, she wasn't about to say it didn't matter. Money—scraped together from gigs in filthy pubs, busking on the street, and even selling her first guitar—was what had allowed her to go to Copenhagen, to the festival, with her mandolin in hand, and play that first gig that really mattered. The one where Jay had seen her, and asked her to come to *their* gig later, a secret afterglow sort of thing for their fans, and pulled her up onstage with him.

She wouldn't argue against money as a motive. But that didn't mean she was just giving in, either.

'*Both* our stars?' she asked sceptically. 'Or is this just an attempt to distract from the fact that ticket sales were trailing off with every tour review, up until the moment Jay kissed me onstage, so now you want us to fleece our fans by lying to them?'

'Of course not!' Kevin sounded far more offended than Daisy thought was reasonable, since that had totally been his actual suggestion. 'I want to use this interest to bring your music to *new* fans, that's all!'

From the tilt of Jay's eyebrows, Daisy was

betting he didn't believe him either. But he also seemed willing to give Kevin's plan a shot. 'How, exactly?'

'Well, now.' Kevin took a seat in the front row of the auditorium and motioned for the two of them to do the same, except then they'd be sitting in a boring row unable to really look at each other, so Daisy ignored him and settled onto the floor, her back against the stage instead. Jay, of course, did as he was told and sat beside Kevin.

'We've got a break in the tour schedule coming up, as I'm sure you both know.'

Did she ever. Daisy had been *living* for this break for the last seven days, ever since the incident with the bus, the muddy back-country road, and the cow, that had led to performing on practically no sleep.

It wasn't that Daisy didn't like touring— well, actually, there was an argument to be made for that, too. But she *loved* performing. Sharing her music with people who actually wanted to listen. Making music with like-minded friends. That was what she lived for.

Sharing a tour bus with five blokes, at least one of whom snored, was not. Neither was dealing with the press, doing interviews, smiling all the time, and living in each other's pockets.

The moving around she was okay with— she'd never been particularly attached to any place anyhow. But she'd like at least a little time to see the places they stopped, beyond the venues and dressing rooms.

And she would *kill* for just twenty-four hours alone, without anyone trying to talk to her.

The break in the schedule was all that stood between her and some sort of furious meltdown that she'd probably end up taking out on poor, placid, miserable Jay. Of course, after the engagement thing with Pamela, he might deserve it.

'Yep,' Jay said to Kevin, his tone wary. 'Three weeks for me to focus on writing the new album, right?'

'I thought we could use this break to capitalise on this fabulous publicity,' Kevin went on, oblivious to Jay's frown and Daisy's suddenly murderous thoughts. 'Of course you'll want to work on the album, but how about working with Daisy, writing a few more duets, since they're what seem to be going down so well right now?'

'More duets,' Jay repeated flatly.

Daisy got the impression he could read between the lines as well as she could. What Kevin meant was, *You can't even perform right now, Jay, let alone write. No one is talking about the music anyway. Let me give you Daisy to distract them all.*

Except she wasn't something that could just be *given* like that. Not like a new watch, or a million dollars, or even an Italian villa…

Kevin continued, regardless. 'And while you're at it, we could set up some public engagements for the two of you as a couple, a few high-profile appearances, maybe even a trip to a jeweller's…'

He left it hanging, as if it were just a suggestion, but Daisy knew from experience that it was nothing of the sort. The label got what the label wanted, and Jay was a far bigger star than she ever hoped to be.

If Kevin thought he could use her to save Dept 135 from Jay's blue period, he would, in a heartbeat.

Well, tough. She signed up to play music and sing her songs. Not to get fake engaged to some superstar. She'd probably get death threats from his teenage fans, for a start.

'Sorry, no can do,' she said as breezily as possible to hide her fury. 'I've…just found out I've been left some property in Italy, and need to spend the next three weeks there sorting that out.'

There. Problem solved.

'Italy?' Kevin's brow wrinkled as he obviously tried to make sense of Daisy's statement. Which, Jay knew, would be difficult, since it made basically no sense at all.

Or at least, not a lot more than Kevin's current plan to marry the pair of them off for the publicity.

Except, in the context of the reviews, the ticket sales and the terrible tour, that made *perfect* sense.

Dept 135 fan? Don't look over there at

those nasty reviews—look at this photo of Jay kissing a pretty girl!

But just because it made sense didn't mean he was comfortable with it. And he knew for a fact that Daisy wouldn't be.

'Yeah,' Daisy responded nonchalantly, despite the fact that Jay was almost certain she was about to launch into some audacious lying. 'My great-aunt. Lovely woman. I'll miss her so much. But she left me her cottage in Italy to remember her by. And so...' she sniffed, mostly for effect, Jay suspected '... I was planning on spending the break there, sorting out the details.'

Daisy was a terrible liar, but somehow Kevin seemed to be buying it. Probably he was mostly afraid of backlash for not being suitably sympathetic in Daisy's time of great—and probably fictional—loss.

'I'm so sorry, Daisy,' he said, with too much conviction for it to be authentic. 'Of course you must go to Italy. We'll work something out.' The phone in his hand started ringing, and he held it up. 'Sorry, must take this. I'll be right back.'

Jay waited until he was out of earshot and then, knowing that Kevin had never been less than ten minutes on a phone call in his life, turned to Daisy.

'What the hell? I thought you just said it was probably a scam. And now there's a Great-Aunt Felicia or whatever?'

'Felicia! That's a great name for her. Thanks, Jay.' Daisy beamed at him, obviously not mourning the loss of her imaginary aunt one bit. 'It's the details that really sell a lie, right?'

It's not having the worst poker face in history that really helps, he thought, but didn't say.

He quite liked that Daisy was rubbish at lying. He'd been lied to enough in his life already. At least he could be reasonably sure that Daisy would never get away with lying to him.

'But why are we lying to Kevin?' he asked, uncomfortably aware that he was complicit here too. He knew there was no Felicia, but he hadn't called Daisy out in front of Kevin. And he knew he probably wouldn't when the manager returned, either, even though he should.

Daisy gave him a blank look, as if it should be totally obvious. 'Um…because I actually *want* a break from this tour?'

Jay shrugged. 'We'll get one either way. I mean, there are no gigs planned for the next three weeks. Did you have plans that are more important than hanging around parties and writing music with me?'

It occurred to him, probably a little late, that she might. That there might be some guy, or some girl, waiting for her to finish touring and come home to them. Daisy didn't talk about her private life much. At this point, he knew more about her fictional great-aunt than any of her actual family.

She spoke of her friends, Aubrey and Jessica, sometimes, but Jay got the impression that they were scattered around the globe and dealing with their own stuff. But maybe Daisy had planned to go visit one of them?

He could sympathise for wanting to get away and back to the people she cared about; normally he'd feel the same way.

When there was a break in the tour schedule, he and Harry tended to head home to Cheshire to see their mum. But right now, he couldn't take three weeks of his mother lamenting the loss of the love of his life, as if Milli had died rather than just walked out on him.

In his family, true love was for life, just as it had been for his parents. His mum and dad had fallen hard for each other the first day they met, married two months later, and stayed happy and in love until the day his dad died of a heart attack, when Jay was seventeen. His mum had never even contemplated the idea of marrying again. 'Your dad was it for me,' was all she'd say when he or Harry suggested dating. 'I had love. I don't need another poor imitation of it at my time of life.'

That was why he'd always been so cagey about introducing girlfriends to his family too soon. But when he was on the cover of every glossy magazine with Milli, keeping things under wraps had been a little tricky.

But this wasn't about Milli. It was about Daisy, and the album he needed to write.

Because Kevin was right: he needed her help if he was going to shake this funk and write something worth listening to. Which meant he needed to persuade her to forget Aunt Felicia, or whatever she really had planned.

Daisy pulled a face. 'Yes, I had plans. Me, a hotel room, and no people asking me questions or needing me to smile for the next three weeks. Seriously, Jay, if I have to stay on show I'm going to blow a fuse at just the wrong moment. Probably with the wrong person. I'll ruin everything, I know I will.'

Jay hid a smile. For all that Daisy performed onstage as if every moment she lived was for her fans, and for all the engaging and extroverted interviews she gave, he'd long suspected it was all an act. At her heart, Daisy was *not* a people person. Hence the snappy and sulky behaviour over the last week or two. She needed some alone time.

He recognised it easily enough; his brother Harry was the same. Jay tended to be more energised by spending time with people, although he'd withdrawn a lot since the break-up with Milli. Harry, however, could only ever enjoy the company of others for so long before he'd need some serious solitude to find his equilibrium again.

Daisy was like Harry. And even if she wasn't planning on spending three weeks in a scam cottage in Italy, she *did* need time away from the tour. So as a responsible mentor figure he'd back her up on that.

'Okay, fine. We'll go with the cottage story. Rest in peace Great-Aunt Felicia, and all that. But Kevin's going to want to know what we're going to do about the album.'

And so was he.

For all his claims of being able to write on tour, Jay knew he wasn't in the right place mentally to do it *and* keep gigging. Plus it was hard to write love songs when he was still mentally reliving what had gone wrong with the only woman he'd ever actually loved.

Even if the love story had been more one-sided than he'd thought.

Daisy's shoulders slumped. 'Yeah. Well, maybe I can just take a week and then we'll get onto it?'

She sounded about as enthusiastic at the prospect of them writing love songs together as he was. But he had obligations, contracts. Fans. Somehow, he had to find a way to get past this writing slump—and Daisy was the best idea he had.

Before he could answer, Kevin returned from his phone call, beaming.

'All sorted, kids! Jay, you're going to go to Italy with Daisy. Kills two birds with one cottage and all that.' Jay shot Daisy an incredulous look, seeing it mirrored on her face. 'You can work on the album together, the media can write about your romantic break away, and Daisy can sort out her inheritance issues at the same time!'

He looked so pleased with himself to have come up with the solution, Jay didn't have the heart to tell him there might not even *be* a cottage. And that even if there was,

Daisy wasn't going to go for pretending to be his girlfriend. One way or another, they were going to have to come up with a solution to this.

But apparently not right now.

Daisy grabbed her stuff, slung her mandolin over her back, and flashed them both a patently false smile. 'Well, in that case, I'll leave you two to decide the rest of my life for me while I go and get some sleep.'

And then she was gone.

Kevin frowned. 'She must really be grieving her aunt,' he said. 'She's normally so happy.'

Jay considered enlightening him as to Daisy's *actual* nature, but decided it probably wasn't worth the time it would take.

'Yeah, that must be it,' he said instead. 'I'll talk to her later, figure something out.'

After she'd calmed down. And in the meantime, he was going to talk to the only stable and sensible person he knew on this tour.

His brother, Harry.

CHAPTER THREE

DAISY SLAMMED ONTO the tour bus, glad that for once it was empty apart from the driver, who was on his phone up front in the cab. She needed to be away from people—especially Kevin.

One thing was abundantly clear to her—she didn't hold enough bargaining chips here to get what she wanted. But wasn't that always the case? It just meant she had to pick her battles. Figure out what she needed most and fight for that—even if it meant giving in on the parts that mattered less to her.

And what she needed most was to get away from this tour.

Flopping onto her bunk, she pulled out her phone. One of the reasons her friendship with Aubrey and Jessica worked so well was that neither of them expected all that much from her. They didn't expect her to be free for a night out when she just needed to be alone. They didn't complain when it took her a few hours—or days— to respond to messages, because she just wasn't in a people place right then.

Daisy liked people—honestly, she did. She just liked them on her own terms.

She thought that Jessica and Aubrey got it. Jessica had a natural gift for connection with others, but she was also generally happiest safely between the covers of a book—well, until she decided to accept the chance to go to New York and interview for a new job, anyway. And while Aubrey was far more extroverted than either of them, after a serious health scare, she hated being fussed over by her loving—but overbearing—brothers, so she got it when Daisy said she was just peopled out.

Now, lying flat on her back on the surprisingly comfortable bunk, she checked her messages, knowing there would probably be something from one or both of them to their message group. She'd texted the group last night to tell them about the solicitor and the cottage, and she was interested to hear what they had to say on the matter.

A cottage? In Italy? Awesome!

Just reading Aubrey's reply made Daisy smile. She could almost hear her friend saying it in her broad Aussie accent.

Italy is totally on my bucket list. But who could have left it to you?

There was nothing from Jessica, which was a surprise. Normally, Daisy would expect her to weigh in with a note about caution, being careful and taking her time. Jessica was always suspicious of change, which was why persuading her to go to New York and find out more about the job had been such a challenge. But she needed it, Daisy knew—and knew that Aubrey agreed too. Jessica had suffered a heartbreaking tragedy years ago that had shrunk her world right down to her small-town life and the books she read. But Jessica was such a friendly, loving soul, she deserved more than to just play it safe her whole life.

Daisy liked to think that she and Aubrey had helped show her that in getting her to accept the New York offer.

That music festival in Copenhagen had given Daisy more than her shot at a serious music career. It had given her friends—a family, almost. She relied on Aubrey and Jessica in a way she'd never been able to rely on her blood relations. They listened to her, gave her advice, helped her stay on the right path. And she knew they only ever had her best interests at heart, which was a lot more than she could say for her actual family.

The day they'd met, at the Annual Ascot Music Festival, had been the day before she'd met Jay and the band. That one festival had given her a future she'd never imagined until then—a successful music career *and* two best friends she could rely on.

They'd come together to save a dog called Max, but once they'd deposited the dog's owner, Viv, and Max at the hospital, the girls hadn't gone their separate ways. They'd stayed up chatting that night, learning about each other's lives. Aubrey and Jessica had come to her gig the next day, had been there when she stepped offstage to cheer her and celebrate with her.

And they'd been there with her, virtually at least, every step of the way since.

Jessica was still silent, but Aubrey was typing again, Daisy could see from the screen. She waited to hear what her friend had to say before responding.

And, speaking of awesome opportunities, guess what? Someone has GIVEN me the money to take the round the world trip I always planned! Just given it to me! Like a lottery win!

Daisy's whole body went cold. Of course she could understand why Aubrey was excited, but this seemed like just one too many coincidences to her.

She wrote back.

Wait. They just gave you the money? How did you find out about it?

This solicitor guy came to my house and told me. There's paperwork, bank transfer details, everything. It's REAL, Daisy!

And that doesn't seem a little…weird to you?

No weirder than someone leaving you a cottage. Or Jessica getting the chance at her dream job in New York, totally out of the blue.

Daisy waited a moment.

Hang on…do you think they're connected?

Daisy had known Aubrey would catch on quickly. She typed on…

I can't see how they could not be. I mean, it's just too much of a coincidence, right? You get the one thing you wanted most, ever since you fell sick—the chance to finish your grand tour trip. And Jessica gets exactly what she needs—the opportunity to step outside her safe little world and try out her dream job.

And you get a cottage in Italy.

Daisy had to admit that part didn't make much sense.

I guess I already have my dream—I'm an actual musician.

With a number one hit! Have I mentioned lately how much I love that song?

Yes.

Daisy knew she was blushing, could feel the heat in her cheeks even though there was no one there to see it. She still couldn't believe that she, Daisy Mulligan from Liverpool, had an actual hit single. What would all those teachers who'd dismissed her dreams as impossible say about her now? Not that she planned on going back to find out.

She typed again, bringing the conversation back to what really mattered.

The point is, all three of us have received mysterious but incredibly generous gifts or offers in the last month. Remember, Jessica's job interview wasn't just for her dream job, it involved days in New York too. What company interviews like that?

Not that Daisy had any idea of what job interviews in New York looked like. Hers had tended to be more of the *Can you pull a pint? Great, you're hired!* variety, back when she'd been serving behind bars rather than playing in front of them. Most of them had barely even checked she was eighteen, which had honestly been just as well when she'd been starting out.

Aubrey had replied.

They've got to be connected. But the only thing the three of us have in common is...

Viv.

Daisy finished the thought for her.

Could the older lady they'd helped in Copenhagen two years ago really be behind their gifts? And, if so, why on earth would she do it? Finding a missing dog didn't earn this kind of a reward.

Daisy could almost understand Jessica and Aubrey's gifts—everyone loved Jessica, and it was so obvious she needed to step outside her safe bubble and find actual happiness, not just contentment. And Aubrey…she'd had such a rough time of it with her illness that of course she deserved to finish her bucket-list trip now she was well again.

But why on earth would Viv give Daisy a cottage? She already had everything she needed.

Aubrey had sent another message.

Let me do some research. See what I can figure out. In the meantime…you'd better go see about this Italian cottage of yours!

Daisy typed back.

Looks like I might not have much choice. Kevin wants me and Jay to head there during the break in the tour schedule. We get to write new songs for the album while also pretending we're on a romantic getaway, since he's practically got us engaged in the press now.

I saw that! Well, it might be a good opportunity, Daise.

How?

There was a long pause before Aubrey's reply came through, as if she was thinking exactly how to phrase it.

You've been…kind of tense about the tour lately, right? I mean, some days your messages sound like you're not enjoying playing at all, and that's not you.

Daisy frowned at the screen, but the sad thing was Aubrey was right.

Maybe this cottage is your chance to get away from it all for a bit and figure out where you want to go next. I mean, maybe that's why Viv sent it to you now. You've already achieved your dreams, so maybe it's time to dream some new ones.

And Jay going with me? How is that helpful?

Gives you something pretty to look at while you're dreaming!

Even in her rotten mood, Daisy couldn't help but laugh at that. Trust Aubrey to find a silver lining to everything.

Harry was exactly where Jay had expected to find him—in the dressing room, lovingly polishing his favourite guitar. Harry had rituals and routines he employed to get him through every performance, and it was rare that he let anything or anybody distract him from them.

Jay just hoped he'd be willing to be distracted today.

'So, I understand congratulations are in order,' Harry said without looking up as Jay entered the room. 'Shall I email Mum and ask her to courier Gran's ring over?'

'Kevin wants us to go ring shopping and get photographed doing it, actually,' Jay replied, morosely.

Harry's head jerked up. 'Wait. You're letting *Kevin* plan the proposal? No way. You need someone with a smidge of romance in their soul. Kevin's heart was replaced with sales figures years ago.'

'Since this pretend relationship is all about sales figures, that sounds about right.' Sighing, Jay sank down into the chair opposite his brother, and watched as he ran the cloth over the instrument.

Harry clicked his tongue. 'Shame, really. If you'd just get engaged, Mum would stop worrying that you've lost your one true love and throw herself into the wedding planning. She might even get off my back about finding a nice young man to settle down with.'

'If she had Daisy as her daughter-in-law she'd have much bigger problems than your love life, you mean,' Jay shot back.

He couldn't ever quite shake the vague guilt he felt about dragging Harry into all of this. Yes, his brother loved making music as much as he did, but Harry would have been as happy as a session musician, or even music teacher, as he was as a member of one of the biggest bands to come out of the UK in years. And while he was sure his brother enjoyed the lifestyle and the money, he knew it came at a cost for Harry.

Love.

Starting the band had been Jay's idea. Getting out and gigging, finding an agent, signing with the label…it had all been Jay. He'd dragged Harry along with him every step of the way, and he suspected that one of the main reasons Harry had gone along with it was because he knew that music was Jay's coping strategy. Throwing himself into forming the band had been how he'd coped with their father's sudden, unexpected death. Just as forcing them all out on tour had been helping him cope with Milli leaving. Until now.

'What love life?' Harry scoffed. 'Your

imaginary romance is more alive than my love life.'

'You could always try going out on a date,' Jay pointed out. 'Then maybe Mum would get off your back. You know she just worries about you being alone.' She'd had true love, and she was determined that her boys should find the same. It was kind of exhausting, Jay had to admit.

'What, you want me to sign up to some dating app and find a new guy to ask out in every city we play in?' Harry shook his head. 'Whatever would Kevin say?'

'Kevin would be fine with it, as long as you were—'

'Discreet?' Harry interrupted.

'I was going to say happy,' Jay replied.

His brother didn't look convinced. And Jay knew he wasn't entirely wrong. The band had an image, and a lot of fans—most of them female. Harry coming out as gay would probably win him some new ones, but Jay knew they'd take a hit from the girls who fancied him most. Not that he cared about that, not if it meant Harry was able to relax and be himself.

But Harry's answer was the same as always.

'I'll tell you again. I don't want the press picking over my personal life until there's something worth picking at. I don't want them watching me every time I talk to a guy, wondering if he's the one for me. When there's something—or someone, I guess—to tell, I'll tell the world, I promise. Right now, I'm happier being a man of mystery. Unlike yourself.'

Groaning, Jay ran a hand over his forehead. 'You haven't even heard the worst of it yet.'

'Worse than having Daisy Mulligan as a sister-in-law?' Harry looked thoughtful. 'Although, actually, that wouldn't be all that bad. She and I could hide out together at big family events and avoid people. She'd probably remember to bring the good alcohol with her, too.'

'You realise I'm not *actually* proposing

to her, right?' Jay asked. 'Whatever the papers—and Kevin—think.'

'What does *she* think?' Harry raised his
eyebrows at him and put the guitar on its
stand to give Jay his full attention. 'I mean,
all this talk about diamonds and a girl could
get ideas...'

Jay barked a laugh. 'Not Daisy. All she
wants is to get away from all of us and not
have to deal with people for a while.'

'I know how she feels.' Harry stretched
his arms over his head. 'I'm going to go see
Mum, then spend two weeks at the cabin,
I think. Out by the lake, just the fish for
company...'

'Well, don't forget to come back for that
awards ceremony in Rome, right?' Harry's
cabin was the one thing he'd bought with
the proceeds of their first platinum album.
'Kevin won't be happy if you miss that.'

'Ah, no one will notice if I'm there or
not,' Harry teased. 'Not with you there with
Daisy on your arm, sporting some giant
rock on her left hand.'

'I was hoping that if you went I wouldn't

have to. But I suppose at least we'll be in the right country,' Jay mused.

Harry frowned. 'You're going to Italy?'

'That's what I came here to tell you.' Jay explained about the curious cottage Daisy might have been left, and how they were supposed to spend the next few weeks there writing love songs.

'Sounds cosy,' Harry commented.

'Sounds more like she might murder me in my sleep if I get on her nerves. She really is on edge right now.' He shook his head. 'I know I'm meant to be her mentor and what have you, but I don't know *what* to do with her when she gets like this.'

'Then maybe this is exactly what you both need.' Harry tilted his head as he looked at his brother, and Jay had the uncomfortable sensation of being studied, observed, like a scientific specimen. Like Harry was trying to make sense of him.

'What do you mean?'

'Well, like you say, Daisy's at the end of her temper and needs some time away before she's allowed out in public again, right?

And you…well. Maybe you could do with some downtime too. All this gossip about your fake relationship with Daisy is one thing, but it doesn't change the fact that you're not actually over your *last* relationship yet, does it?'

Jay thought about lying, about telling Harry that he was completely over Milli, that he barely even thought about her these days. But Harry knew him too well for him to believe that.

Although even his brother didn't know the real reason the break-up was hanging over his head. It wasn't as their mum thought, that Milli was his one true love and he'd never fall for another woman. It might have been, if Jay hadn't realised the truth—as much as he had believed himself in love with Milli, the woman he'd thought he loved didn't really exist.

Because for Milli, their relationship was as much a publicity stunt as his fake relationship with Daisy.

If their love affair had never been real for Milli, how could he really have been in love with her in the first place? *That* was the question that was messing with his head. What made love real?

But he didn't want to get into that with Harry now.

'I guess some time out of the public eye wouldn't be the worst thing in the world,' he admitted instead. Maybe away from all the chaos of the tour and the cameras, he could get his head around what had happened with Milli, and how he was going to move on.

'You going somewhere, Jay?' Nico, their drummer, swung through the doorway and dropped into a spare chair, followed by their bassist, Benji.

'He's whisking Daisy away to Italy for a romantic break,' Harry said, wiggling his eyebrows.

Nico rolled his eyes. 'Yeah, well, try and write some decent new songs while you're there, yeah? I'm getting bored of hearing the two of you singing the same damn duet every night.'

'I'll see what we can do,' Jay promised

dryly. 'You guys don't mind me skipping out during the break in the tour schedule?' They didn't always spend the time together, and Harry would be in Cheshire then at the cabin in Scotland anyway, but as their frontman, their leader even, Jay felt an obligation to check.

Nico shook his head. 'You keeping out of the limelight for a few weeks gives the rest of us a chance to shine for once. That's fine by me.'

'Plus Daisy might help lighten you up a little bit,' Benji put in. 'No offence or anything, but you've been a miserable bugger so far this tour.'

Jay looked to Harry for confirmation; his brother winced and nodded. 'I wasn't going to put it quite that bluntly but…yeah.'

'Daisy's fun,' Benji said, with a shrug.

'Daisy's gorgeous,' Nico added. 'You'll just have to make sure you don't end up back here engaged for real.'

The memory of that one, impulsive kiss they'd shared onstage flared up in his head, his blood warming instantly. Jay forced himself to think of the diamond ring still sitting in the bottom of his suitcase instead. The one he'd bought for Milli, before she called everything off.

He'd been burnt that way before, no way he'd be stupid enough to fall for it again. Not when, this time, he knew right from the start that nothing about his connection with Daisy was real, however fantastic that brief kiss had felt.

'I don't think we need to worry about that,' he said dryly. 'Now, I need to go find Kevin before the show. And Daisy.'

Apparently, they had travel plans to make.

CHAPTER FOUR

'Is THIS EVEN a real airport?' Daisy asked as she wobbled off the tiny plane that had flown them from Rome to…wherever the hell they were now. The back of beyond, as far as she could tell.

So much for her plans to spend the tour break in a plush hotel with room service on tap. All she could see here was hills, scrub land, and a tiny control building next to the airstrip their minute plane had landed on.

'It's more of a private airfield, I think,' Jay replied, squinting in the sunshine. 'But Kevin said there should be a car waiting for us…'

How Kevin had got so involved in her escape from the public eye, Daisy still wasn't entirely sure. But ever since Jay had come and found her on the bus and declared that he thought they should go to Italy together, things seemed to have been spiralling out of her control.

She'd started off well, putting her foot down on the things that mattered. Yes, Jay could come to Italy with her but only on the proviso that they were going together to write music, nothing else. Jay had agreed easily to that condition, as had Kevin— the latter with a rather suspicious wink that made Daisy doubt he was *actually* going along with her wishes.

But she was escaping, and writing music wasn't exactly a hardship.

Of course, at that point, Kevin had taken over everything.

The solicitor, Mr Mayhew, had been delighted to be dealing with Kevin, someone who seemed to have considerably more understanding of property and law than Daisy. And at least Kevin's involvement had reassured her that it definitely wasn't a scam— although it had also involved some very confusing conversations about Great-Aunt Felicia.

The more she learned about her strange inheritance, though, the more Daisy became convinced that Viv, the lady they'd helped in Copenhagen two years ago, had to be behind it. Apart from anything else, there was literally no one else in the world—apart from Jessica and Aubrey—who would give her anything.

Which was kind of sad, when she thought about it.

But if Viv was responsible, then it linked in with Jessica and Aubrey's recent good fortunes too. Jessica was still radio silent, but Aubrey had been doing some digging, and had sent her a photo of Vivian Ascot, the billionaire owner of Ascot Industries— who coincidentally sponsored the music festival they'd all attended in Copenhagen. The photo was an old one, the woman's face shaded by a large sun hat, but if she squinted, Daisy could definitely see their Viv in the image.

But while she'd been preoccupied with the mystery of why Viv would give her a house, Kevin seemed to have organised everything else. Including the flight from the States, where they were touring, to Italy—and the transfer on the terrifyingly small plane to this airstrip in the middle of nowhere.

And the driver, holding a handwritten sign with their names on that, on closer inspection, appeared to be written on the back of a birthday card. He leaned against a dusty car, his eyes half closed in the sunshine.

Not quite the limos Jay was used to these days, she was sure, but still more than she expected when she travelled, even now.

The driver's English was limited but, by joint pointing at maps on their phones, Daisy managed to confirm where they were going, while Jay loaded their cases into the boot of the car. She slid into the back seat beside him, and held onto the door as the car jerked forward towards what could only charitably be called a road.

'So, have you seen photos of this place?' Jay asked as they bumped along.

Daisy nodded. 'One or two.' She pulled out her phone again to show him the pictures Mr Mayhew had sent her. They showed a single-storey, stone-built cottage with a bright blue door, set against a backdrop of rolling Italian countryside—green and lush in parts, yellow in others, with tall, thin trees jutting up into the sky all around.

'It looks beautiful,' Jay said, swiping through the images. 'Perfect place to get away from everyone for a few weeks.'

'Everyone except you.' Daisy pocketed the phone again. 'Mr Mayhew said that there's a village at the bottom of the hill, so hopefully we can get supplies and such there. There might even be a bar or two.'

'Sounds fun.' The words were right, but Daisy couldn't help but notice that Jay didn't sound exactly excited at the prospect.

'I'm sorry you got forced to come here with me.' Not that spending three weeks in the middle of nowhere with Jay was her first choice for the tour break, either. But it had to beat playing up to the press and pretending to be engaged to him in public.

Jay shook his head and gave her a half-smile. 'Honestly, you're doing me a favour.

I mean, even Harry suggested it would be good for me.'

'Because we'd work on some new songs together?' Something she knew Jay had been avoiding ever since the tour started. She hadn't brought it up because, quite frankly, performing every night, zigzagging across the USA in the tour bus, and giving regular interviews at each stop had drained any creativity right out of her, and she imagined it was the same for Jay. But she knew as well as he did that the label had expectations.

'Partly. Mostly I think he hoped it might shake me out of the funk I've been in since—' He broke off suddenly, but Daisy didn't need him to finish the sentence, anyway.

Since Milli, that was what he was going to say. Since the woman he loved walked out on him and their future in the most public, humiliating way she could manage. Really, who dumped someone in a social-media video, anyway?

'Well, if nothing else, you won't have to

deal with Pamela Pearson hounding you about whether you've bought me an engagement ring yet,' she said cheerfully. She'd seen the depressive moods Jay could sink into when too many reminders of Milli got the better of him—like the time her new video had been playing on the huge TV screen in the tour bus's living area when they got back after a gig. Or when one interviewer had only asked questions about the demise of their relationship for a full five minutes.

Yeah, the less said about Milli Masters, the better, in Daisy's opinion.

'Harry offered to call Mum and ask her to send Grandma's ring over for you,' Jay replied, obviously relieved at the change of subject. 'I mean, it's a tiny speck of a diamond hidden in a gold band, but if you want it...'

Daisy pulled a face. 'I'll pass, thanks. I'm kind of hoping they'll have all forgotten about it by the time we get back.'

'Does it bother you?' Jay asked, curiosity

colouring his tone. 'All this fake relationship stuff, I mean?'

Daisy shrugged. 'A bit. I mean, you and I know it isn't real. But I don't like living a lie.'

'Yeah, I know what you mean.' Jay sounded a little uncomfortable with it all too, Daisy realised. Why? Surely this was just part of the fame game, right? Especially for him, being such a huge star. People had speculated that his relationship with Milli was just for the cameras too, but given his reaction to the ending of it, she guessed not.

'Does it bother *you*?' she asked. 'I mean, it's basically just Kevin spreading gossip, right?' Except Jay had been the one to start the engagement rumour in the first place. And the one to start everything by kissing her during that duet.

And now they were writing more. God, people really were going to start talking. Was that what Jay wanted?

'It doesn't bother me, exactly,' Jay said slowly. 'Not when I know that it's part of the game. More it's just weird, you know? My mum finds it baffling. Like, why would anyone pretend to be in love when they could just find someone to fall in love with for real?'

'Your mum makes a good point,' Daisy admitted. Not that she was looking for love. From what she'd seen, love mostly led to heartbreak. Music was a much safer option.

'But I guess…everything we do is a performance, right?' Jay went on. 'The songs we write—they might have some of us in them, but they're still not a word-for-word rendition of our thoughts.'

'And when we're up onstage… I'm not Daisy Mulligan from Liverpool, exactly. I'm Daisy Mulligan, rock star. And that's something different.' Sometimes, that person felt a world away from the real her. Daisy suspected that might be why she enjoyed playing her so much.

Up onstage, she wasn't the Daisy who everyone agreed would never amount to anything. The useless daughter who wasn't enough to stop her mum from leaving, or the student voted most likely to drop out. Up onstage, she could prove them all wrong—but it never really felt like her.

'I guess it's the same when we give interviews.' Jay sounded thoughtful. 'We present ourselves a certain way.'

'Like a job interview,' Daisy put in. 'Not that I really know much about those.'

'Yeah. So do you reckon pretending to be in love is just like pretending you speak fluent Spanish on your CV?'

Daisy laughed. 'My teachers were impressed I ever managed to learn to speak English properly, never mind a foreign language. But yeah, I guess it's the same principle. You just have to hope you never get caught out—like someone asking you to translate at an important meeting or something.'

'Or in our case, asking us to kiss in front of the cameras.'

Daisy shot him a look. 'That didn't exactly seem to be a problem for you last time.' She'd meant it as an accusation, but it came out a little breathier than she'd intended.

And Jay didn't look exactly apologetic, either. One eyebrow raised suggestively over his green eyes, while amusement played around his lips. And for a moment—just a second, really—she found herself wondering what it would be like to kiss them. To kiss Jay Barwell, world's sexiest man. Not a fake kiss for the crowds and the cameras. A *real* kiss.

Then the car bashed into another bump in the criminally uneven road, just when she'd finally let go of the seat cushion, and lurched sideways, sending her tumbling towards Jay's lap.

Strong arms caught her—stronger than he could have got from just playing guitar, but she supposed that was why Jay had requested that the back of the tour bus be set up as a workout zone, rather than the luxurious master bedroom he could have commanded.

A strange, long-forgotten flutter started deep in her belly. Suddenly, every single time she'd touched Jay was racing through her mind like a film reel. They'd shaken hands when they met, she remembered. Hugged outside that club in London when Kevin offered to sign her. He'd slung an arm around her shoulder like one of the guys often enough as they took a bow on-stage. Then there was that kiss…that she really wasn't thinking about. And just that afternoon he'd put his hand to the small of her back as he guided her up the rickety steps to the tiny plane from Rome, his palm radiating heat. But none of it had felt like this. Not…close. Close enough that she could breathe in his aftershave, feel the heat of his body against hers.

She wanted to reach out and squeeze those muscles—but she didn't. If Kevin was determined to play up some fake affair between them in the press the last thing she wanted to do was complicate that with actual lust or—God forbid—feelings. Any fake relationship was definitely just a marketing strategy.

So as the car righted itself, Daisy pulled

away and muttered, 'Sorry,' before tucking herself back into the far corner of the car, glancing out of the window for a distraction. They bumped over a few more potholes in the road—Daisy held tightly to the seat this time to avoid a repeat performance—while they climbed the hill. As they crested it, a small, tumbledown villa came into view. One with the same stone walls and tiled roof as the photos she'd been sent, although this one was in far worse condition. And as the path curved around, she realised it sat right at the top of a cliff, practically on the edge, looking out over the ocean. It must be a typical construction style for houses in the area, she reasoned.

Until she realised that the road they were on stopped at the edge of the cliff. At the faded and peeling blue front door of the falling-down villa. And her heart sank all the way down into the waves below.

Jay was still considering the strange jolt of attraction that had sparked through him as Daisy crashed into his arms, when the car started to slow. Mostly because it was so unexpected. He'd barely felt a connection to anyone, in any way, since Milli—and certainly not that sharp flare of something akin to lust that had taken over his body as she'd pressed against him. Even the night he'd kissed her onstage, he'd been feeling more relief that the crowd were enjoying the show again than lust for the woman attached to the lips he was kissing.

Daisy's gorgeous, he heard Nico's voice repeating in his head. And yes, of course, she was. He wasn't blind, and he sang love songs to her every night onstage. Of course he'd noticed that she was beautiful. Perhaps not in the conventional way that Milli was, with her honey-blonde hair and perfect curves, but in a different, vibrant way that was all Daisy.

He just hadn't thought that beauty was anything he needed to worry about.

Except now he realised he was alone with it for the next three weeks. And it appeared that certain parts of his anatomy were suddenly very aware of what that might possibly mean if, and it was a long shot, Daisy had felt that same spark.

A *very* long shot, he told himself, given that she was currently staring out of the window at the villa outside and paying him no attention at all.

Wait. Villa. Did that mean they were there? He craned his neck to see past her. No, this couldn't be it. The villa in the photos Daisy had shown him had been bright, well-kept and welcoming. This place looked as though the walls might just cave in if he glanced at them wrong.

Except the car had stopped. And the driver was getting out...

'This is it?' he asked, trying not to sound incredulous, and knowing that he'd failed.

'Apparently so.' Jay couldn't quite read the look on Daisy's face as she turned to him. It wasn't quite disappointed. More... resigned? As if she should have known this would happen. 'Sorry.' The apology was short and quiet, as if she wasn't used to giving them.

Actually, from what he knew of Daisy, she wasn't.

The driver had already unloaded their bags from the back of the car, and was hanging around smiling broadly. Jay resisted the urge to ask if he was sure this was the place, and handed over a tip instead, unsurprised when the man jumped back behind the steering wheel and scarpered.

'I guess we'd better see what we're dealing with, then,' Daisy said, glaring at the peeling paint on the door as if it had done her personal harm.

Jay followed gingerly behind her.

When he'd heard 'villa in Italy' he'd imagined spending this break in the schedule relaxing by the pool, sipping cocktails, strumming his guitar under a cypress tree, partaking of the local specialities at a trattoria in the village…and maybe writing a song or two with Daisy.

Instead, it looked as if he'd be searching for a hardware shop to buy a hard hat, and trying to avoid being brained by falling masonry.

'We could just call Kevin and head back to the States,' he suggested as he lingered in the doorway. At least the door frame seemed sturdy. It might be the safest place in the building.

'And spend three weeks smiling for the camera and pretending to be wildly in love? No, thanks.' Daisy shook her head a little too violently, sending a cloud of dust flying up from a nearby table. 'Kevin would have us married by Elvis in Vegas before the tour started up again.'

'True.' Jay took in the very dusty dust sheets covering the furniture and tried to decide which was the worst fate—Elvis, or death by dust inhalation. Thank God Harry hadn't come. It would have played merry hell with his asthma.

Squinting up at the ceiling, he decided it wasn't going to fall down *imminently*, so stepped inside.

The villa's front door opened onto one main room, filled with sheet-covered chairs, tables and—from the shape under the fabric—bookcases. No TV as far as he could see. One door led through to another room at the back that, from the glimpse he could get through the open doorway, was the kitchen. Another opening led to a hall-way with several doors off it.

'Shall we explore?' he asked, raising an eyebrow at Daisy. She looked so grumpy about the whole thing, Jay decided he'd have to tease her out of it. Make it all a game, an adventure—the way he used to have to do for Harry when they were kids, and his little brother got into a sulk over something.

'If you're sure you want to risk it,' Daisy replied, looking doubtfully towards a bro-ken window in the open-plan living area.

'Well, then, if madam will follow me?' He held out his arm, elbow crooked. Daisy rolled her eyes, but took it. 'Through the authentically rustic front door we find the spacious living area. With—' he whipped off a few dust sheets and tried not to succumb to the threatened coughing fit

'—ample seating for the occupants and their friends. There are myriad entertainment options built in,' he added as another dust sheet fell to reveal shelves of tatty paperbacks—all in Italian—two jigsaw puzzles and a Scrabble set in a beat up box. 'And incredible views through the very clear windows.' Clear in that half the glass was missing. The view part was true, though. From where the villa sat, they could look out of windows one side that showed them the rolling ocean, down below the cliff, and out over the hills and cypress trees on the other.

Actually, if the place weren't in such disrepair, it would be a fantastic little bolt-hole.

Daisy was smiling now, even if she looked as if she was trying not to, so Jay swept her towards the kitchen to continue his tour.

'In here we find a state-of-the-art kitchen, ideal for making, uh…' He looked around him for inspiration but, quite honestly, he wasn't even sure he'd know how to turn the stove on. At home he was an okay cook—he could keep himself fed, at least. But the range cooker here was a mystery to him. Then he spotted the answer. 'Cocktails!' he finished, whipping out a dusty bottle of limoncello from the back of the open shelving.

'Well, thank God for that.' Daisy grabbed the bottle from him and set about opening it. 'Finally something is going right.' She took a swig, pulled a face, and passed it to him.

He copied the motion. 'Sickly sweet.' He pressed his lips together. 'And sticky.'

'Sounds like Milli Masters' last tour,' Daisy joked, then shot him an uncertain look, as if she wasn't sure if he was ready to joke about her yet.

He hadn't been, Jay knew. But here, now, with Italian liquor, a wreck of a holiday villa, and Daisy, he thought he might be. Just.

He grinned, to show her it was okay, and actually watched the tension leave her body. She was so slight, every movement showed in her stance—the stress and frustration in her jaw, the disappointment in her shoulders, the determination in her legs, planted firmly on the floor. She was fascinating to read, Jay realised. A whole story wrapped up in a woman.

He wondered if he'd get to read it, this next few weeks.

Stealing the bottle back, Daisy took another swig of limoncello. 'Come on,' she said. 'Bedrooms next.'

And for a flash of a second as she said the word 'bedrooms', Jay remembered her body against his in the car, and couldn't help but think what a shame it was they needed two.

Yep. Definitely getting over the whole Milli fiasco at last, it seemed. Harry would be so proud.

Jay grabbed the limoncello, took one last gulp, swore, and followed her towards the other side of the villa.

Daisy woke up the next morning to a drip from the ceiling that landed right on her forehead, and the feeling that she should have known better. Yes, Jessica might get offered her dream job in New York, and

Aubrey might get a life-changing amount of money to complete the bucket-list trip she'd had to cancel when she got sick—but that didn't mean that she, Daisy Mulligan, screw-up extraordinaire, would actually get something good too.

Things like just being given a holiday villa in Italy didn't happen to people like her. In fact, she'd obviously used up her entire family's share of good luck by getting signed to the label in the first place. Asking for anything more was just being greedy.

And from that point of view, it was almost a relief that the cottage was a disaster zone. Because if it hadn't been, she'd have spent the next three weeks waiting for the other shoe to drop. As it was, she could just accept that this was another episode in the entertaining but disastrous life of Daisy Mulligan, and spend three weeks swigging limoncello from the bottle and pretending it wasn't happening.

Or she *could*. If she hadn't brought Jay along for the ride.

Now, she had to make this work. Otherwise, Jay would drag her back Stateside to parade her around as his girlfriend, and she knew how that would end. She'd screw it up. She'd lose her temper, say the wrong thing to the wrong person, get filmed doing something stupid. When it was just her, no one much cared what idiocy she got up to, or how much trouble her sharp mouth got her into. But if she were Jay Barwell's fiancée…a whole different level of scrutiny and interest and expectation followed.

Which meant she had to find a way to make this cottage habitable for the next three weeks.

They'd found the bedrooms easily enough the night before—they just followed the scent of mildew. There were four of them, tucked away at the back of the cottage. Two with double beds, one with a twin, and one with a very saggy set of bunk beds. Jay had chivalrously insisted on her taking the one with the biggest bed—and actual windows. He'd taken the other double, using one of the dust sheets to cover over a missing pane.

Her head spinning from the limoncello and the journey, Daisy had collapsed into bed, grateful that at least the bed linens had been packed away in plastic covers that didn't seem to have been eaten by mice or anything. But she hadn't slept, not for hours, her brain spinning as she tried to understand why Viv—if it was Viv—would have left her this wreck of a place.

This morning, however, she knew there was somewhere more important to focus her attention. She had the villa, so now she had to make it liveable. Which meant she needed help, because the last time she'd held a hammer she'd almost lost a finger. And that would be very bad for her future as a guitarist.

She couldn't imagine that Jay was any handier with power tools, so that meant finding someone who was. She just hoped that the people in the village at the bottom of the hill spoke English, because her Italian was non-existent.

The plumbing had proved as erratic as the rest of the place the night before, so

Daisy skipped a shower in favour of a quick wash, dressed in jeans and a flowy tunic top that she thought would suit the weather, and headed out. Creeping past Jay's room, she heard his familiar snores, and figured she had some time to figure this all out before he inevitably woke up and demanded to be returned to civilisation.

At the worst, Daisy reasoned as she headed down the steep hill towards the village, nestled in the valley, there might be a hotel or something they could check into for a couple of weeks. Or Jay could, anyway. All the way out here it was unlikely that Kevin was going to stop by and check they really were fake loved up in Italy, wasn't it?

But the closer she got to the village, the more her hotel dreams started to fade. It was definitely more of a hamlet than a village, she decided—just a cluster of houses scattered in between the trees and scrub. Did it even have any shops? There was no food at the villa, just that rogue bottle of lemon liquor. If there wasn't a shop nearby they were really going to have to find some way to hire a car or something. Or decamp to the nearest city and admit defeat.

No. Daisy couldn't quite explain the defiance that rose up in her at the idea, but she knew it was about more than not wanting to have to pretend to be Jay's girlfriend in public for the next three weeks.

Maybe it was just her natural stubbornness rising to the fore. She'd been given a house and she was damn well going to live in it. Or perhaps it was the feeling that this was some kind of test—one she was expected to fail. And while she'd never been a grade A student, if someone—even herself—told Daisy she couldn't do something, she would bloody well do it. She'd seen the disbelief in the taxi driver's eyes when they actually got out of the car and went into the villa. And she knew that Jay was just waiting for her to come to her senses and retreat to a hotel or something.

Well, he'd be waiting a long time for *that.* Her grandmother always said she didn't have any sense, anyway.

But she did have an appetite. Her stomach

gave a loud growl as she reached the edge of the hamlet, and she hoped against hope there'd be a café or something.

It was still quite early, but the place was starting to come to life. People chatted on the street, kids raced past. And actually, now she was down there in the midst of it, it seemed bigger than it had from the top of the hill. More vibrant.

Spotting a few café tables set out on the pavement, Daisy made a beeline for them, grateful for Jay remembering that they needed to change dollars for euros at the airport. She had a feeling that this place wouldn't take cards.

The café, if she could call it that, seemed to be someone's front room. It was set into a traditionally built house in a row of identical ones, the only difference being that this house had the front windows thrown open and a temporary counter balanced on the sill. Presumably it was anchored somehow, although Daisy couldn't see how, as it was laden with pastries and cakes. Behind the counter stood a beautiful, curvy brunette woman in a red dress, laughing as she prepared espressos and handed over plates loaded with bread and jam, or filled pastries or biscuits.

There were a couple of empty tables in amongst the occupied ones, but most people seemed happiest standing up at the counter chatting, espressos in hand. Looking at the beautiful, laughing woman, Daisy supposed she didn't blame them. She seemed warm and welcoming in a way that, so far, Italy really hadn't been. All the things that no one would ever call Daisy. Also, she was hot as hell—even Daisy could appreciate that.

She just hoped she spoke English.

CHAPTER FIVE

JAY AWOKE ALONE, which was not unusual, and to silence, which was. After months on tour he was used to the everyday sounds of the tour bus, or the rare hotel they got to spend the night in. To Harry banging on his bunk to wake him up, or room service arriving with breakfast. Or even his own fast breathing after another alcohol-induced nightmare. Never silence, though.

Then he opened his eyes fully, took in the disaster of a bedroom he was sleeping in, and remembered everything. Especially the limoncello, as his head began to pound.

Daisy was nowhere to be found, so he washed up as best as he could with the creaking plumbing, pulled on some clean clothes, and headed out in search of her—and breakfast.

Outside, the day was already warm and sultry, the sort of heat that made his muscles lazy and his brain switch off. He ambled down the hill towards the village, his hands in his pockets, the start of something that might be a melody humming in his head, just out of reach. He knew better than to try and catch it, though. Any time he tried to force the music, or lyrics, it always fell apart on paper. If he just waited, let his subconscious develop it without any interference from him, eventually it would be ready for him to take and make into something real.

Something he could sing, and play. Maybe even with Daisy.

The village itself seemed bustling with activity, and Jay followed his nose towards a café serving espresso—clearly what he needed to kick-start his day. Conveniently, it also led him to Daisy, who appeared to be having a very convoluted conversation in sign language and one-syllable words with the confused-looking woman behind the counter.

Jay had assumed that the ability to order coffee in any language was a prerequisite for a touring musician, but apparently not.

'Need some help? What do you want?' he asked, sliding in beside Daisy at the counter and flashing the Italian woman serving a smile. 'Cappuccino? Espresso?'

Daisy just glared at him, so he decided to just make the call. He was pretty sure he'd seen her drinking black coffee on tour, so he went with that.

'Un Americano e un cappuccino, per favore,' he said, and the café owner smiled and nodded with obvious relief, and headed off to make their coffees.

Jay turned to Daisy, who raised her coffee cup and drank from it ostentatiously.

'You…already had coffee. So what was the problem?'

'I was *trying* to ask her if she knew any tradespeople who might be able to help me fix up the villa.' Her eyebrows lowered over her coffee cup as she glared at him again. 'Until you bumbled in here trying to save me or whatever.'

'Help,' Jay countered. 'I was trying to help. Which I see you do not actually need in respect of coffee. But I'll see what I can do with the other stuff, too.'

'You speak Italian?' Daisy asked disbelievingly. 'Like, not just ordering-coffee Italian?'

'Your faith in me is astounding,' he muttered as he tried to call up his very rusty language skills. 'I actually lived in Italy for a few months on my gap year, working in a pizzeria. Had to pick up at least *some* of the language.' But that had been a good few years ago now, and even then it had been more to do with getting paid on time and spending his money on beers, not home repairs.

Daisy was staring at him as if he'd come down from another planet, although he had no idea why.

The barista returned with their coffees, and Jay took his cappuccino gratefully. Then, in halting Italian, he asked her about local builders or tradespeople, hoping he hadn't mangled the words too badly.

She looked puzzled for a moment, then her face cleared. She pointed up to the hill where Daisy's villa sat, and spoke in a torrent of fast-flowing Italian. Jay clung onto any words he recognised, nodding along as he tried to make sense of it all. He'd told Daisy he could speak Italian, and he was damned if he was going to be proven wrong now.

Then the woman beckoned to a couple of men sipping espressos at a table nearby, and they stood and moved closer, joining in the rapid-fire conversation. Beside him, Daisy's eyes were wider than he'd ever seen them, and he could tell she liked not knowing what was going on as little as she'd enjoyed him playing male saviour for her over the coffee.

Finally, one of the burly guys that had joined them turned to Jay. 'You are English?' he asked, thankfully *in* English. 'You own the villa on the hill?'

'She does,' Jay answered, pointing to Daisy. 'Do you think you could help us fix it up?'

The men looked doubtfully at each other, then shrugged. 'Maybe. We will see.'

Then they put down their empty coffee cups and walked away.

Jay scraped together enough of his Italian to ask the barista, 'Where are they going?'

She shrugged, too, as she cleared the empty cups. 'To work,' she replied, in Italian. 'They will come to the villa when they are done.'

'Right. Okay, then.' He relayed the information to Daisy, who looked as doubtful about this method of hiring contractors as he was. Still, it didn't look as if they had a lot of choice but to wait.

'In that case, I guess we might as well look at finding some food?' she suggested as they finished their coffees and waved goodbye to the barista. 'Also, you know, thanks for sorting that.'

Jay barked a laugh. 'I'm not sure I'd call it exactly sorted. Besides, I'm staying in that villa too, remember? I want to get it fixed up as badly as you do.'

Daisy gave him a sideways look as they

strolled along the streets of the village. 'I kind of expected you to demand we move to a hotel.'

He almost missed a step as he realised that had never crossed his mind since he'd woken up that morning. Why not? It was the obvious solution to the problem of the crumbling villa.

Except…he knew hotels. He'd spent half his life in them, it felt like. And this… hanging out with Daisy, ordering coffees and sipping them in the square, knowing that no one knew or cared who they were, or if they were really together or just faking…he liked that.

He wasn't ready to give that up just yet.

'This is more of an adventure,' he said eventually. 'Come on. Let's find a shop and stock up. I'm starving, and I don't want to have to walk up and down that hill every time I fancy a coffee.'

After a little more wandering between the houses, they found a row of old-fashioned shops selling variously fruit and veg, deli meats and sausages, and freshly baked bread that smelled divine. Along with a more familiar convenience store to provide butter, milk and eggs—plus a couple of bottles of wine—they were able to stock up on pretty much all the essentials of life, and stuff them into the backpack Daisy had brought along, plus a couple of extra shopping bags.

The walk back *up* the hill was rather less relaxing than the walk down it had been, and conversation was little between them as they fought the incline. How was it he could jump around onstage singing until his lungs screamed, six nights a week for months on end, without feeling this out of shape?

At the top of the hill, they paused to catch their breath for a minute, before continuing towards the villa.

'We should make a list,' Daisy said suddenly as they approached the front door. 'Of everything that needs doing to the villa, in case those builders really do come up here.'

'Good idea.' Jay pushed open the peeling front door and stared at the sight before him. A goat—brown and white and with tiny little horns—stood in the middle of the living area, staring back at him. He swung the door open a little wider so Daisy could see. 'We can start with whichever broken door or window let the damn goat in.'

The list—written after they'd chased the goat outside by first roaring at it, then laughing hysterically, which it seemed to find much scarier—was seven pages long. Seven pages of things that were wrong with this inheritance of hers.

Why had Viv given the others perfect, no-strings gifts—and lumbered her with a money pit? Daisy couldn't figure it out. But at the same time, it seemed perfectly in keeping with what she expected from her life.

Things didn't come for free. Fairy godmothers didn't just shower people with gifts—at least, not people like Daisy. She had to fight and scratch for everything she wanted in this life, and even then she had to cling onto it with a death grip, or else it would just melt away.

That was how life worked. She'd seen it clearly enough before she was even sixteen, and had it repeated plenty of times since. Her teachers might disagree, but even Daisy eventually learned her lessons when they were *that* obvious.

Besides, her mother had been her biggest teacher—maybe not in reading or writing, but in how the world worked. She'd taught her that at the age of six, when she'd crept into her room in tears and told Daisy that she couldn't do it any more. She couldn't give up her own life, her own dreams, for a man who didn't appreciate her, who kept her down and forced her into a life she hated. One where all that mattered was whether she had dinner on the table and kept quiet during the football. She loved Daisy, she promised as she laid her old mandolin beside her on the bed, hitching her own guitar onto her back. But she had to chase her own dreams too.

Daisy had learned an important lesson

when she'd woken up to find her mother gone: she wasn't enough to make anyone stay. And dreams mattered more than love.

She'd learned it again at fifteen when her stepmother had kicked her out for the first time, after another argument over what mattered more—babysitting her little brothers so her dad and stepmum could go to the pub and spend the grocery money again, or practising with her band so they could play some paid gigs.

She'd come back and done as she was told that time. But she'd started planning, too.

Daisy knew what she needed to know to survive. First, that she had to get out and chase her own future, because she could be damn sure that no one else would do it for her. Secondly, that she didn't want to rely on anybody else to get it. She'd seen too many older girls from the neighbourhood settle for guys who weren't right for them, just because they had a flat, or a job. She'd watched her dad and stepmum relying on hand-outs from the government just to live, after Dad lost another job. She'd seen her best friend and band mate give up what she wanted—what they both wanted— because she fell in love, and her new boyfriend didn't like her playing in a band, let alone chasing big-time success.

Daisy wouldn't be like them. Not any more. She had made it, at last, and that meant she didn't need to rely on anyone else. She wasn't going to give up *anything*. Love, family…all that stuff came with a cost. And, as she'd learned since she left home and started to make it on her own, so did everything else. It was better to know what the cost was upfront.

Which was why she was almost glad that the villa was a wreck. At least that made *sense*. Viv had obviously needed to get rid of it for tax reasons, or couldn't be bothered doing it up herself, so had passed it off under the appearance of a gift. That, she could understand. It was like those smarmy guys from the record company who talked up all the ways they wanted to help her build her career—mentorships, support, opportunities. Daisy knew what they really meant.

We want to make money from you. Here's what we'll give you so you don't notice we're taking advantage.

She always knew when people were taking advantage, because people were always taking advantage. She just made sure that what she got in return was worth enough to her.

In this case, the villa was an escape, and that was worth a lot. When it came to her career, music had always given her the same thing—the chance to escape home, to escape poverty, to escape fading away to nothing. The rest of it was beside the point.

Except, somehow, it had also given her Jay, sitting beside her at the rustic wooden kitchen table, chewing the end of his pencil as he added to the list.

'Is "fix the heating" on there?' Daisy asked, shivering. 'Or is that more of a "fix the broken windows" issue?' The day had almost gone, and all they'd really done was potter around the village, buy food, scare a goat and cook a late lunch/early dinner that they'd eaten with one of the bottles of wine they'd bought. It had been nice—a break from the list, at least. But now the sun was sinking outside, although given the time of year she imagined it would take a few more hours to actually dip under the horizon.

Jay looked up, his eyes shining in the fading sunlight. 'Cold? That, at least, I can do something about.'

Dropping his pencil onto the table, he crossed the room to the fireplace, and poked around for a minute or two. Daisy looked on, apprehensively.

'Are you sure we should mess around with that? There might be squirrels nesting in the chimney or something. Maybe another goat.'

Jay turned to her with an amused look. 'You're really not all that comfortable with wildlife, are you?'

'Are you?'

He shrugged. 'I grew up next door to a farm.'

That must have been nice, Daisy supposed, although she couldn't actually imagine it. 'I grew up in the city. I know rats and pigeons and that's about it. Maybe an urban fox or something.'

'And you're right, the chimney probably needs cleaning.' He gave her an assessing look. 'But if you were up for it, we could build a campfire outside? I saw a fire pit out the back earlier.'

'Can't be any colder out there than in here,' Daisy decided. 'Come on.'

Outside, Daisy settled onto a wooden seat, while Jay set about fetching firewood from the store. She watched, enthralled, as he laid the fire, then lit it, coaxing the flames to life. She tried to remember if she'd ever sat by a real fire, out in the countryside—rather than an accidental fire with sirens and engines, like the one at her school that time. She didn't think so.

She knew, in many ways, she was a lot younger than Jay. In years, maybe only six or so. But there were so many experiences out in the world that he'd had and she'd never even dreamt of. Like university—or a gap year in Italy.

Of course, she'd had a lot of experiences she guessed he hadn't either. Like sleeping on London's streets, or running away from home. She wasn't naive, never that. But despite growing up probably only fifty miles apart, their lives had been so totally different—until that festival in Copenhagen threw them together.

She wondered what the label had given him to keep him in the job of her mentor. She couldn't imagine he was doing it for fun. It was clear now what Kevin and the label got out of it—her under control, some great publicity via their new fake relationship, and maybe even some songs, if they ever got around to writing any.

She just couldn't figure out what Jay got.

Once the fire was roaring away, Jay stood up and headed back for the house.

'Where are you going?' Daisy asked, panicked. She *definitely* didn't want to be left alone in charge of wild flames.

He shot her an amused look. 'I'll be right

back. Try not to set the whole hilltop ablaze while I'm gone.'

Yeah, that made her feel loads better.

True to his word, he was back moments later, his guitar slung on his back in its case, her mandolin under his arm, and gripping one of his jumpers. He tossed the jumper into her lap. 'Put that on until you warm up.'

She should argue, Daisy was sure. But she *was* cold, and her packing had been more for sultry summer Italy, plus her ubiquitous leather jacket, neither of which were serving her particularly well right now.

She tugged the jumper over her head, breathing in the familiar scent of Jay. Wait. When had that become familiar? On the tour, or when she'd crashed into him in the car…? She wasn't sure. She just knew that for the rest of her life, she'd be able to pick his clothing out of a pile by scent alone.

She was clearly a woman of many talents, most of them less than profitable. It was just as well she could sing, play, and pull a mean pint, or she'd be worthless to the world.

'Are we writing?' she asked, taking the mandolin from him. The instrument felt so familiar in her hands, her fingers smoothing over the wood and finding the strings instinctively, plucking and tuning it without thought.

Jay shook his head. 'Let's save that for the morning. I just thought it might be fun to play together.'

Daisy looked down at her hands, plucking the strings lightly as she refined the tuning. It had been so long since making music had just been about having *fun*, if it ever had been. For her, music had been her way out—something she had that others didn't, something that she could use to escape her home, her family, and find something *more*, as her mum had tried to do.

Tried, and failed. But she didn't like to dwell on that part.

Nobody really knew what had happened to her mother. But Daisy knew what *hadn't* happened. She hadn't found the success she craved, or else everyone would know her name, her music.

Like they were starting to know Daisy's.

Without her really thinking about it, her fingers began picking out a melody—an old song, a familiar one. One that seemed to have followed her around her whole life. Had her mother sung it, before she left? Maybe. Daisy couldn't remember.

But Jay knew it, too. Because he started playing along—all the right chords, moving with her tune, adding depth and dance to the music.

There were words, too. About luck and stars and moonlight and possibility. As the sun sank behind the hill, Daisy's hands flew over the strings instinctively as she opened her mouth and began to sing, Jay's lower voice joining her on the harmonies.

And for the first time in months, she felt as if she might be exactly where she was supposed to be. Even if she wasn't chasing anything, for once.

Someone was hammering something.

Jay had kind of assumed the banging was just inside his head, after last night's wine and the smoke from the fire—plus the last three hours of trying to drag a tune he couldn't quite hear out of his head. Why was it so easy to make music when it didn't matter, when they could sing and play anything they dreamt of or remembered—but so damn hard to do it when it was important? When they needed to write the songs they'd promised Kevin they'd work on during the break?

'What the hell is that noise?' Daisy scrunched her nose up and dropped her pen on the floor.

Right. The hammering.

'I'll go and find out.' Jay put down the guitar he'd barely played all morning anyway and headed outside.

The source of the banging quickly became apparent: the builders they'd met the day before in the village square had taken out one of the broken window frames.

'We finished our job,' the one with the better English said. 'So now we are here. We fix this.' He gestured to the window. Or possibly the whole house. And the goat that was still loitering on the edge of the cliff.

'Great. Thanks. Um...*grazie*.' See? He hadn't forgotten *all* his Italian.

The builder nodded. 'This place has been empty too long. It is good to see it being cared for again. We're glad to help.'

'We're very, very glad you're helping too.'

Leaving them to their work and heading back inside, he filled Daisy in on the latest developments.

'So they're...fixing my house? I mean, I haven't paid them a deposit or anything. They haven't even given me a quote. They're just...fixing it?' There was a small line between her eyebrows that made her look like a confused child.

'Apparently so. I mean, I expect they'll want paying at some point, but...' He shrugged. They both knew that money wasn't exactly an issue for him—and she couldn't exactly be broke either. He knew what she was getting paid for this tour, and that was before he factored in the income from a number-one record. She could afford it, and if she couldn't, he would.

But Daisy didn't seem quite so relaxed.

'I need to give them money.' She jumped up from where she was sitting, cross-legged on the floor, and headed for the door. Jay watched her go, all fire and fury, and wondered which of her many triggers he had hit this time.

He wasn't under any illusions that Daisy had enjoyed the same happy childhood and opportunities that he had in his life. He didn't know her story—had never felt close enough to her to ask before—but that much was obvious from the barriers she threw up whenever anyone *did* ask about her past. Or her present for that matter. Anything personal, and Daisy wrapped that leather jacket of hers around her like armour.

Her usual weapons of deflection were sarcasm, her incredibly sharp tongue, and a blank, incredulous look that left the object of her attention feeling like the stupidest person on the planet.

He'd been the subject of that look too often already for him to push for more answers.

Except...

He'd sat with her last night and sung to the stars and felt more himself than he had since long before Milli. He'd come here with her to this place. And if they had three weeks together, just them, he couldn't see that distance lasting. She'd managed to maintain it on the tour, even living on a bus together. But this was different, somehow. There was no Harry to run interference, no busy schedule to keep them too rushed to think, no fans to sign autographs for every night, no interviews to give, and no Kevin with that damn tablet scheduling their every second.

It was just the two of them.

And two Italian builders.

And a goat.

Belatedly, Jay followed Daisy outside and found her trying to hand euros to the bemused builders.

'We fix this. *Then* you pay us,' one of them was saying.

'Are you sure?' Daisy sounded so confused, so uncertain, that Jay had to step in.

'Just say *grazie*, and we can get back to work,' he said, taking her arm and tugging her back towards the front door.

'*Grazie!*' Daisy called back over her shoulder.

'Paying people after the job is done isn't exactly unusual, you know,' he pointed out as they headed back inside. 'What's the issue?'

Daisy gave an uncomfortable shrug. 'I don't know. Just…they don't know us at all. They don't have to be here—it's Sunday, for crying out loud. They could be home, with their families.'

'Maybe they need the work,' Jay suggested. 'Or maybe they saw how desperately we needed the help. One of them said to me that this place had been empty a long time. I think they're happy that someone *wanted* to fix it.'

Daisy looked thoughtful. 'When you mentioned it yesterday, and the woman at the café pointed to the hill…they all seemed kind of excited then, too.'

'I guess this place has been abandoned and crumbling a while, but they still consider it part of their village.'

'Or they know who owns it,' Daisy said suddenly. '*That* would make sense.'

'*You* own it,' Jay pointed out.

'Well, yeah, *now* I do. But they don't know that. I bet they know who owned it before me, though.'

'And do *you* know?' It had been a mystery, hadn't it? Some weird legacy from a relative she hadn't even known she possessed. At least, that was what Jay had believed. Watching Daisy squirm now though, he thought otherwise. 'I take it that it wasn't Great-Aunt Felicia?'

She rolled her eyes. 'There is no Great-Aunt Felicia. You know that.'

'So who gave you the cottage?'

'I think… I think it might have been Viv Ascot.'

Jay's eyebrows jumped so high he felt them hit his hairline. Of all the answers he'd expected—if he'd expected any at all—that was probably bottom of the list.

'Multimillionaire heiress and business-woman Viv Ascot?' he asked, just to be sure.

Daisy nodded. 'I met her at the same festival I met you. My friends Jessica and Aubrey and I—well, they weren't my friends then, because we'd only just met, but they are now—we helped find her dog when she lost it and took her to hospital because she'd hurt her ankle chasing him. We exchanged social-media details, but didn't really hear much from her again. But now Aubrey and Jessica have both received dream gifts this summer too, and I...'

'Got the crumbling villa in Italy,' Jay finished for her, still trying to process the story she was telling him. 'But why do you think it's Viv Ascot?'

'Because she is literally the only thing the three of us have in common, apart from being female. Different nationalities, different careers, *very* different personalities.

The only thing that links us is that we all helped Viv.'

'Huh.' He supposed that made a sort of sense. 'What did the others get?'

'Jessica got the chance at a dream job in New York, which is brilliant, because she'd really shrunk her world to just her hometown since we met in Copenhagen.' That little frown was back, just a small line between her eyebrows. God help him, but it was adorable. 'Although we haven't actually heard from her since she got there. Hopefully that means she's having too much fun, not...' She shook her head. 'Anyway. Aubrey messaged me just before we left for Italy. She's been gifted the money to complete her dream trip of a lifetime, touring Europe. She had started when we met, but then she got sick and had to go home and it was kind of terrifying for a while. But now she's better she can have all the adventures she always dreamed of.'

'Sounds to me like they both got exactly what they needed.'

'Yep. That's what I figured.' Jay was

pretty sure he knew exactly what was causing the disappointment in her voice.

'And you can't figure out why Viv Ascot would think you needed this place?' he asked.

'Can you?' She looked up at him, eyebrows raised. He wasn't entirely sure if it was a rhetorical question, but he didn't get the chance to answer it anyway.

Without warning, a huge crash sounded from the side of the house, followed by some fast-flowing Italian that Jay was pretty sure consisted entirely of words he wouldn't repeat to his mother. There was a panicked bleat, and then the goat jumped in through the open window, almost landing on Daisy's guitar before she yanked it out of the way.

'Maybe she thought you needed a quiet, secluded place to write some duets with a friend?' he suggested weakly.

Daisy just raised her eyebrows a little higher.

He sighed. 'Yeah. Come on, this isn't working. I've got a better idea.'

CHAPTER SIX

'WHERE ARE WE GOING?' Daisy's guitar bumped against her back in its soft case as she followed Jay along the cliff top.

While she was glad to be away from marauding goats and the builders possibly destroying her house, she couldn't quite understand how this hike through the Italian countryside was going to help them with the writing-songs issue.

'We're not going anywhere,' Jay said, without looking back.

Daisy looked down at her feet, still moving across the yellowing grass. 'I'm pretty sure we are.'

Glancing over his shoulder, Jay rolled his eyes at her. 'I mean, we're not going anywhere in particular. I always find my best song ideas come to me when I'm walking. Don't you?'

'No.' Her best ideas came in that place between sleeping and waking, when her creativity was awake but the rest of her brain—the part that told her she couldn't do this, that no one would want to hear it—hadn't stirred yet.

'Huh.' Jay stopped walking and turned towards her. 'I guess…we never talked about how we were going to do this—write together, I mean.'

The duet they'd performed every night of the tour so far was one Jay had written before they'd even met—the song that she'd joined them onstage for in Copenhagen. It hadn't been intended as a duet, as such, but it had been an easy enough job to add in some harmonies, switch around who sang which lines and so on. Kevin had suggested they refine it for the tour, and they'd done it in an afternoon.

Coming up with a whole song—or two or three or four—from scratch, together, was an entirely different proposition.

'I've never written a song with another person before,' she admitted. Mostly she liked to have total control over her music. The idea of letting Jay in was kind of scary in the first place. But that was part of the cost of her success, she knew that. 'How do you do it?'

Looking thoughtful, Jay sat down a metre or so away from the edge of the cliff, stretching his legs out on the parched grass. The sun was warm and sultry overhead, and away from the building work and the goat the cliff top was amazingly peaceful. Daisy followed suit and sat too, wondering how long it had been since she'd heard such quiet.

As a musician her life was always full of noise—with melody and harmony, with percussion and the twang of strings, with cheering crowds and sound engineers and managers and the band, with the purr of the tour bus. Out here, there was none of that.

Even the music in her head was quiet. Which would be a nice change, perhaps, if she didn't need to hear it to write songs.

'Do you have to sit so close to the edge?' Jay asked, his voice a little strained.

Daisy looked down at her hand, next to the cliff drop. She'd sat facing him, but closer to the cliff, her guitar on the ground beside her, and from the look on his face he wasn't entirely comfortable with it.

She couldn't help herself. With a wicked grin she twisted so her feet dangled off the edge of the cliff and she was looking out over the water. There was a thin strip of sand below them, with a few walkers and sunbathers enjoying the beach. If she leaned forward, Daisy could watch them all going about their summer day…

Arms wrapped tight around her waist and tugged her back, her bottom scraping against the grass as she pulled up her feet to stop them catching on the rock of the cliff. Still grinning, she took a moment to realise that her little joke now meant that she was held tight against Jay's broad chest, the scent of him filling her lungs again, and the heat of his body was definitely not un-noticed by her own.

Maybe she hadn't thought this through. Like most things in her life.

'Are you trying to give me a heart attack?' he almost growled in her ear as he moved them away from the edge, and the sound ricocheted through her, leaving tingly wanting feelings wherever it hit.

Yeah. Definitely hadn't thought this through.

She was so tight against him that, as they tumbled onto their backs together, she could feel his heart beating—too fast. He really had been scared, and for *her*. Huh.

She wanted to make a joke, a 'didn't know you cared,' or a sarcastic comment or *something* that sounded like her, in this place and time where she felt less like Daisy Mulligan than ever.

But what actually came out of her mouth was a question, soft and without mocking. Totally unlike her at all.

'You don't like heights, huh?'

Jay shuddered. 'Hate them. I fell out of a tree when I was about six, and I've avoided them ever since. Better than Harry, at least—he jumped off the roof of the barn next door when he was ten. Lucky for him, he landed on a hay bale. I landed on the tree roots and broke my collarbone.'

She winced. 'Ow. Sorry. I didn't mean to scare you.'

It seemed to dawn on him then just how close they were—his arms still wrapped around her waist, his breath against her cheek, their legs tangled together—because his muscles suddenly tensed against her. Daisy, for her part, hadn't been able to ignore their closeness even for a moment.

Or the effect it had on her.

Perhaps pretending to be in love with Jay Barwell wouldn't be so bad, if she got to feel his body against hers like this when they posed together for photos. Maybe they'd even kiss again…

No. That way lay confusion and feelings and issues, and she wasn't even thinking about it. Not when she was lying in his arms, anyway.

Jay's arms fell away when she wriggled out of them, sitting up cross-legged beside him. 'Okay, so now we've established that neither of us are going to fall off the cliff, how about we talk about how we're going to write these songs together?'

Nodding, he sat up too, legs outstretched and leaning back on his hands. 'Yeah. Okay. Um, where do you want to start?'

She threw up her hands. 'I don't know! I've never written with another person before. All my songs…they're just me. And I'm not sure they're exactly what Kevin and the label wants for my next album anyway.'

He gave her a curious look. 'What makes you say that? They wouldn't have asked you to do this with me if they didn't want your sort of music.'

Was he really that naive? 'They asked me to do this with you because they can use it to promote our entirely fictional relationship and therefore the floundering tour.'

Jay leaned closer, a teasing heat in his gaze. 'Ah, but there's only a fake relationship in the first place because people watching us perform together sensed the chemistry between us.'

'Because you kissed me, you mean.' Heat surged through her again at his words, and she forced it back down. 'But that was fake too. Just a performance.'

'Was it?' He held her gaze for a moment too long, her mouth drying out as the look lingered.

She could look away. She *should* look away. He couldn't force her to keep looking into his eyes.

So why did it feel as if he were?

With more effort than it really should have taken, Daisy tore her gaze away. 'You're flirting with me.'

And even though she was trying not to look at him, she must have been watching anyway because she saw the amused smile that curved his lips, and the laughter in his eyes.

Damn her traitorous gaze.

'Isn't that what a fake fiancé is supposed to do?' he asked, too casually. Was he as affected by this conversation as she was? Or was this just his rock-star cool at play?

'You haven't actually fake-proposed to

me yet, you realise. I'm still technically just your fake girlfriend.' And, right in that moment, something more. Something she couldn't put her finger on, and it bothered her.

'Do you want me to?'

'No.'

She didn't want him to pretend to propose to her. She wanted him to kiss her, for real this time.

She'd always preferred to focus on reality rather than make-believe, even as a child. Except…kissing Jay would be just another sort of make-believe, wouldn't it? Pretending that she could be the sort of woman he'd actually have a relationship with—or even just that she was the sort of woman who could manage a functional relationship. Which, she knew from past experience, she was not.

Men always wanted something from her. Sex, of course, but not just that. Money, even when she didn't have any, and even more so now that she did. An in at a club she'd played, or an introduction to her manager, her label. A leg-up in a brutal industry. Or just to share her fame.

Jay already had all those things, but there were others he could want from her. And nobody gave anything for nothing, not even love.

Why was she thinking about love? She needed to be thinking about music.

'I don't want you to fake propose,' she said, firmer this time. 'I want you to help me write a song. So pick up that damn guitar.'

'Yes, ma'am.' Still smiling, Jay reached for the instrument, and Daisy willed her heartbeat back to normal tempo.

Focus on the music. That was all they were there for.

It took them three days to come up with anything approaching a song idea they could work with. In that time, the builders had fixed the windows, and the front door, made a start on some dodgy-looking roof tiles—and Daisy had named the goat.

'She looks like a Genevieve, don't you

think?' she said as she shared her breakfast with the creature on their fifth morning at the villa.

'She looks like a nuisance,' Jay countered. But he had to admit, it amused him to see Daisy—who generally disliked and mistrusted most humans—making friends with a goat.

'Are you ready to get to work?' he asked, watching Genevieve lick pastry crumbs from Daisy's fingers. 'I think we've nearly nailed that first song.'

Daisy pulled a face, but nodded.

Was the face about working or about the song? Either way, Jay shared her sentiments. It wasn't that the song they'd written was no good. It just wasn't…them. Actually, it was more like *fake* them. The song embodiment of the fictional relationship Kevin seemed to have developed for the press.

'It's working like magic!' Kevin had enthused when he'd called the night before. Jay had taken the call in his room, somehow reluctant for Daisy to hear him discussing the fake romance with their manager. 'The photographer I sent to the airport caught a fantastic shot of you with your hand on Daisy's back—you know, loving and protective—and now that photo is *everywhere*. If anyone had any doubts about the two of you before, they certainly don't now. All the gossip sites are talking about your romantic, secluded getaway in Italy!'

'You haven't told any of them where we are, have you?' Jay had asked, sharply.

'Pff! Of course not,' Kevin had replied, and Jay had actually felt a sense of relief— until he'd explained why. 'I don't think Daisy could keep up the facade of *actually* being in love with you in front of the cameras, do you? This way we get all the talk and drama without worrying about Daisy letting on that it isn't real.'

Of course, Kevin didn't have the same concerns about Jay giving the game away. As far as Kevin was concerned, Jay had faked a relationship before, with Milli. Because apparently Jay was the only person involved who *hadn't* realised that relationship wasn't real, until the end.

Which brought him to his current problem. Jay didn't want to write songs about another fake relationship. He wanted to set to music the way Daisy had felt in his arms on that cliff top—as if she might roll over the edge and disappear at any moment if he didn't hold on in just the right way. He wanted to sing about the heat that pulsed through him when she met his gaze, the way his whole body spoke to hers—even if hers wasn't listening.

He wanted to write about what was real. And more than anything else in his world, Jay knew that Daisy was real.

Real and infuriating. Real and insecure. Real and defensive. Real and sarcastic and mean and mocking.

But real.

The only problem was, writing about those things would let on that he'd been *thinking* those things, and he definitely wasn't supposed to be doing that. Their friendship and professional relationship were completely separate from the fake relationship they were supposed to be in, and there was no space between those two worlds for anything else.

Like the desperate need he had to kiss her whenever he let himself look at her lips.

Not thinking about that. Not even to blame himself. After all, if he hadn't kissed her that night onstage, he wouldn't know how surprisingly soft those lips were under his...

Dammit, he was thinking about it again.

They'd taken to working in the main living space, because the sun streamed through the windows almost all day, and they were close to the kettle for coffee in the morning, tea in the afternoon, and near the fridge for alcohol as soon as they decided they weren't getting any more value out of being sober.

This morning, Daisy curled her feet under her on the best chair in the room and pulled her guitar into her lap. On tour, he was used to seeing her mostly in her stage outfits—skinny jeans, logoed vest tops and her favourite leather jacket. Here in Italy she seemed to have lightened up with the weather, favouring flowing skirts with the vest tops instead, or flowy tops with the jeans. The sight of her bare toes—nails painted with unexpected turquoise polish—poking out from under her skirts had been known to distract him for up to half an hour.

God, he was a pathetic individual.

He'd tried telling himself that it was just the proximity, or the music, or the fact that the whole world thought that they were dating. But deep down he knew it wasn't any of those things.

He just wanted Daisy Mulligan. Badly.

'Do you want to go over what we wrote yesterday?' she asked, pulling out a sheaf of notes from the folder on the table.

He should say yes. That was the safe thing for them to do. To go back to fake passion in fake songs about a fake love affair. Just like the songs he'd written for other people to sing, while he was waiting for the band to get their own shot at fame. People like

Milli, singing about forever love and then turning around and leaving their supposed beloved behind. At least he knew how that world worked.

'Let's try something new,' he said, before his brain could talk him out of it.

Daisy looked up, eyebrows raised in surprise, but he could see the excitement in her eyes. She was as bored with that song they'd been labouring over as he was. 'You've got something in mind?'

He hadn't, not really. Nothing beyond a feeling and a few snippets of lines that haunted his sleep at night, and the patches of melody he'd half written in his head walking into the village that first day. But he picked up his guitar anyway. He might be a company man these days, but he still knew how to improvise.

'Maybe something we can work up,' he said. 'I don't know. See what you think. You might hate it.'

But, God, he hoped she didn't.

Gingerly, he strummed a couple of chords before finding his rhythm. Music had always felt like a river to him, flowing through his body as naturally as blood in his veins. He could feel it inside him, working its way to his fingertips and vocal cords, seeking a way out into the world.

His whole life, he'd just had to give himself over to the music and it had come. He hoped that wouldn't fail him now.

As his hands found the melody he'd been searching for, the one that had been writing itself in his subconscious all week, he knew instinctively that this was the song they'd been searching for. And when Daisy picked up her guitar and started playing a counterpoint, a small smile under her closed eyes, brow furrowed with concentration, he knew she felt it too.

But the words. The words just weren't there for him. Harry was more of a lyricist than he was, and for a moment Jay wished his brother were there with him. Then he looked at Daisy again, lost in the music, and changed his mind.

He didn't want to share this moment with anyone else.

As the melody began to repeat, Daisy's warm, husky voice suddenly joined the song—sometimes just vocalising with sounds, sometimes singing actual words, even some complete lines. Jay shifted closer to hear them, to understand them, although they were nothing like complete lyrics. Still, what he could hear only warmed his blood, and his hopes.

'And when you're close, oh, how I feel you. Down deep inside my soul,' she sang.

And Jay couldn't help but wonder if she could sing that with such feeling if she didn't mean it. If it wasn't real.

Unless she's singing about somebody else, you idiot.

He tried to force reason back into his brain and pull away. But then Daisy opened her eyes and her gaze hit his and he just *knew*. She felt it too. Whatever this ridiculously strong pull he felt towards her, whatever it was that just made him want to drag her into his arms and keep her there, safe from the rest of the world, *she felt it too.*

And that changed everything.

His fingers stalled on the strings and Daisy's song faded away until they were sitting in silence, just staring at each other.

Daisy collected herself first, clearing her throat and looking away. 'Uh, I think that could work. Um—'

No. He wasn't going back to that again now. He couldn't, not now he knew.

So instead, he reached out and grabbed her hand, tugging her towards him so she had to look up at him again. And then he leaned in, just those few precious inches, waiting to see if she'd follow his lead in this, as she had with the music.

A pink tongue darted out and swept across her lower lip. She blinked, slow, and he could see the heat in her eyes. Then she moved, just a fraction, closer, closer—

'Mah!' Genevieve bleated loudly in his ear and Jay jerked back, out of the range of goat spit, trying not to swear. And failing.

'Genevieve!' Daisy scolded, but, given how fast she moved away from him, he wondered if he heard a little relief in her voice.

She'd wanted that kiss as much as he had, he'd seen that in her widened pupils, in the pulse thrumming fast at her throat. But she didn't *want* to want it. Why?

That was what he needed to figure out now.

Just one more mystery of Daisy Mulligan.

'Yes, I know, Genevieve. I'm hiding. You don't need to give me that look.'

The goat stared balefully at her regardless, as if she were as disappointed at Daisy's life choices as her family always had been. As if Genevieve hadn't actually been the one to bring her to her senses two days ago anyway.

If it weren't for the damn goat she'd have kissed Jay Barwell. Again. And then, knowing her, she'd have started getting ideas.

She couldn't afford to get ideas about the world's sexiest man.

It was one thing when she was fourteen, believing that her eighteen-year-old boyfriend really meant it when he said he only loved her, when actually he had two other girls on the go at the same time. It was one thing taking up with a twenty-something guy when she was sixteen because he had a room over the pub where she could crash for a while, in return for her affection. And it was one thing falling for a musician who claimed to love her—but loved her talent, and the prospect of sharing in her fame, a hell of a lot more.

People always wanted something in return, that was the rule, and she had to remember it. At least Jay had been upfront about what he wanted—a fake relationship and some songs to boost their flagging tour sales and popularity, plus probably show Milli Masters that he wasn't still wallowing over her leaving him, even if he was.

She couldn't let herself believe, not for a second, that this was about anything else. That it might just be about how badly she'd wanted to kiss him, before Genevieve had intervened.

So she was avoiding him. Because it was easier than dealing with the butterflies in her stomach—and the other feelings some-what lower—every time she met his gaze.

Of course, that made progress on the new songs rather slower. Which she felt bad about; she did. Except…she couldn't move past those long minutes when they'd played together, when the words that needed to go with the beautiful melody he'd written had just come to her, complete in parts and a work in progress in others. Those minutes when she'd known exactly what the song was about, because she could see it in his gaze.

It was about wanting. It was about that pull to a person you knew couldn't be right for you, but that you couldn't stop want-ing all the same. It was about a voice down deep inside saying that this was the one.

Even when he couldn't be.

And she'd known he was thinking the same as her. They were on the same wave-length as surely as they always were on-stage, when they sang to each other in front of hundreds or thousands of people.

Which was why she had to stay away.

'Are you done avoiding me yet?' Jay's voice rang out around the outside walls of the cottage, perfectly audible over the hammering on the roof as Matteo and Lorenzo fixed the roof tiles.

Daisy winced. 'No, not really.'

He came into view around the corner of the villa, skirting Genevieve cautiously, and approached Daisy. 'Tough. I just had a call from Kevin and you're going to have to start talking to me pretty soon.'

'Why?' He didn't ask why she was avoiding him, she realised. Because he already knew. Because he felt the same.

'There's some awards show in Rome I'd hoped we were skipping, but apparently Kevin wants us there. Together.'

'Damn.'

He laughed. 'Is being seen on my arm such a terrible chore?'

'It's more the "dressing up and wearing heels and make-up" part I wasn't looking forward to,' she confessed. 'Plus you know Kevin will probably have an engagement ring waiting ready for me to wear. He probably measured my finger in my sleep on the tour bus.'

Jay shuddered. 'That's worryingly plausible. Actually, Harry offered to bring my gran's engagement ring to the awards if you wanted it. Apparently he really did ask Mum for it while he was at home.'

Daisy recoiled in horror. 'Why would he do that?'

'I think he meant it as a joke.' But even he didn't sound entirely sure.

This was ridiculous. They couldn't carry on like this. They needed to come to some sort of rebalancing here. One that could let them move past this awkwardness and tension and get back to work. And in her experience, only one thing had worked consistently for ruining potential relationships and encouraging men to move on and ignore her.

Getting drunk and sleeping with them.

Jay was an actual rock star. It stood to reason that it would work for him too, right?

Chewing her lip, she tried to figure out how best to suggest it—and if she even wanted to. She *liked* Jay. She wasn't under any illusion that he might be her one and only or anything—they were too different for that, and she didn't believe in all that 'soul mates' stuff anyway. And that was before she got to the part where he was still in love with his all-American, beautiful, successful ex-girlfriend.

But she didn't want to trash the friendship they'd built up, either. They still had to work together, once this was over.

Still, this was the only plan she had—other than hiding out with a goat, which wasn't actually working that well for her.

'Okay. If we need to go back to civilisation and start faking a relationship again, I think we need to do a couple of things first,' she said.

'Like talk about how we almost kissed?' Jay suggested, suddenly closer than she'd thought. Close enough that she could just—

She stepped back. 'Talking is overrated,' she told him, meeting his gaze head-on. 'We need to go and get drunk.'

CHAPTER SEVEN

JAY HAD NO idea exactly what Daisy's plan was here, but so far he was having fun.

The last couple of days had been unbearably awkward. Ever since that almost kiss, Daisy had been keeping her distance, refusing to meet his gaze, acting skittish and un-Daisy-like. He didn't like it. He far preferred her snarky and mocking to this quiet and evasive Daisy.

Fortunately, with her latest suggestion, she seemed to have got back to her old self again.

The village at the bottom of the hill was small, but it did at least boast a bar—one which, so far, they'd discovered had plenty of different sorts of alcohol for them to try. It was a little hole-in-the-wall place, with a barely legible wooden sign over the door.

Jay wasn't sure he'd have even noticed it when they walked past, but it seemed Daisy had a nose for places like this.

'It's the many, many years I spent working in them,' she'd explained, when he'd questioned it.

Taking the beer she'd offered him, he'd done some swift mental arithmetic. 'Years? Did you start bartending in secondary school?'

Daisy just shrugged. 'Places like this aren't so fussy about things like age.'

He wondered now how old she'd been. Seventeen? Sixteen? She couldn't be more than twenty-four now, and he knew she'd been playing around pubs and bars for a few years before he met her in Copenhagen, two years ago.

She'd never talked about her family, he realised. Not once. But now, he wondered where her parents had been when she'd been pulling pints and busking in the streets. Who had looked after her?

He almost didn't want to know the answer.

Now, he leaned across the rustic wood

table, beer bottle in his hand, and asked her, 'Remind me why us getting drunk tonight is going to solve all our problems?' It hadn't made much sense when he was sober, but he suspected that a couple of beers in it might start to be understandable.

'We're too tense around each other.' Daisy talked with her hands a lot, he realised, watching as she waved her beer bottle around. 'We need to loosen up.'

'We're tense because we're trying not to give in and kiss each other.' *Oops.* Apparently the alcohol had loosened his mouth up plenty already.

Daisy's eyes widened a fraction, before she spoke. 'Well, maybe the drinks can help with that too.'

'I don't think every bottle behind that bar would make me want you less.' Hell, he just had no filter at all tonight, did he? 'So you're going to have to explain to me why I shouldn't.'

Her gaze locked on his. 'What makes you think I'm trying to convince you not to?'

Raising one eyebrow, she got to her feet—

not breaking eye contact—and gave him the sort of smile he'd only dreamed of. The sort that sent fire coursing through his veins.

Then she turned and stalked to the bar, leaving him watching her hips sway as she procured them more drinks.

'Why am I not surprised that ordering alcohol is one thing you can do in Italian?' he asked, when she returned with shot glasses for them both.

She laughed, warm and low. 'You know me. Always focussing on what's important.'

He should change the subject from their previous conversation, he knew that. He should get them back to friendly fake boyfriend and girlfriend, to collaborators and colleagues. Mentor and mentee. But the air between them sizzled with potential, with the sort of tension that could just snap at any moment.

He might snap if he didn't do something about it. Either they had to decide to ignore it and hope it went away. Or…

Well. It was the 'or' that had been keeping him awake at night.

'And tonight it was important that you brought me here.' As she sat, he reached across and took her hand, visibly startling her. 'Why, Daisy?'

'Because...' She licked her lower lip again. He wondered if she knew what that did to him, if that was why she did it. Milli would have, he knew. The moment she spotted a weakness in him she homed in on it, exploiting it for all it was worth. But with Daisy...he doubted she even realised she'd done it. 'We need to get past this...thing between us, right? Ever since we wrote that song together—'

'You mean the day we almost kissed,' Jay said, for clarity, and enjoyed watching the slightest hint of pink flush Daisy's cheeks. He'd never imagined that she could blush. He wondered what other parts of her might turn pink with the right attention.

'Yeah.' Her voice was husky on the word, like when she sang deep and full of meaning, and it hit him places even Milli had never quite reached. God, he needed to keep drinking until he stopped thinking about her this way. She'd made it obvious that whatever the attraction between them she didn't intend to do anything about it, which meant he needed to move past it, as she'd suggested.

Except then she said, 'I think we need to have sex.'

It took a lot of effort, but Jay just about managed to not drop his drink, swear loudly, or drag her over the table into his arms in the next instant. Just.

'Is that the alcohol talking?' he asked cautiously. 'Because honestly? I don't see how actually getting to see you naked is going to make me want you any less afterwards.'

'You'd be surprised,' she said, with a wry smile. 'Normally I find that most guys lose interest after they've got what they want from me.'

'I'm not most guys.' He hoped that was true. He definitely knew she was wrong about him losing interest.

She shook her head as if she were shaking away his objections. 'Look, the point is, we need to be able to work together. And we need to be able to pretend that we're a couple. We can't do that if we're flinching every time we touch.'

'Or hiding from each other.'

'Exactly. So we need to get comfortable with each other again. We didn't have this problem on the tour, right? Not even after you, well, kissed me onstage that night.' She rushed the words, as if it would stop him remembering how her lips felt under his. It didn't. 'We just moved past it, right? Probably because we were so busy, and there were so many people around, and you were—'

She broke off, but he knew what she hadn't said. 'I was still wallowing after Milli.'

'Yeah.' Her mouth twisted up into an awkward smile. 'I mean, at least this is a good distraction from that, right?'

'Definitely.' He'd barely thought about Milli since he'd arrived in Italy, while she'd consumed his every waking thought when they were on tour. Until he'd kissed Daisy, anyway. She might have thought they'd moved past it, but for Jay it had felt more like trying to ignore all the strange new feelings it had kicked up in him.

And now, here… It was as if he and Daisy had shifted universes to one where only they existed. Well, them, Genevieve and the builders.

'Plus, people act differently when they've slept together. You can see it just by looking at them.'

He raised an eyebrow. 'So your pitch here is that we should sleep together because then I won't want to do it any more, but Kevin will be happy because more people will believe that we're a real couple?' Because that definitely had to be the shots talking, right?

Daisy leaned forward over the table, low enough that he could see right down her top to the curve of her breasts. 'My pitch is that we should sleep with each other before I actually lose my mind with lust.'

Any blood in his body that was still doing its actual job, rather than just getting overheated, gave up and flooded south.

Jay swallowed down the last of his drink, got to his feet, then held out his hand to Daisy. He didn't care what her logic was, she obviously needed this as much as he did.

And he wasn't letting any damn goat stop him this time.

'Let's get out of here,' he said, and she nodded.

They were halfway out of the door before he remembered about the stupid hill back to the villa. Even then, he didn't let it slow them down for too long.

Daisy laughed, the sound music on the breeze as he dragged her up the winding path. 'Somebody's eager.'

'You have no idea,' he growled. 'I have been *dreaming* of this moment ever since you tumbled into my arms on the car ride up here.'

'Me too,' she whispered, so softly he only just caught it. The admission just made him more desperate, and he picked up speed again. Hell, he'd pick her up and carry her if he had to.

'No, before then,' he corrected himself. If they were being open and honest, he might as well go all the way. He could always blame the alcohol later. 'Since I kissed you onstage, and pretended it was just for show.'

Her only response to that was a small, desperate gasp. Jay smiled and redoubled his efforts to get them home quickly.

Finally, finally, they reached the top of the hill, and then the front door. It was late enough that the builders had finished work and gone home hours ago, and even Genevieve seemed to have found somewhere else to be.

Jay pulled Daisy close, spinning her so her back was against the front door. He'd intended to give her an opportunity to back out, to change her mind. But as he saw her there, flushed in the fading sunlight, her short black hair just falling against her cheekbone, her skin glowing, he realised something.

'I haven't even kissed you properly yet. Not without an audience. I'm half crazed for you, and I haven't even kissed you.' How could it be she had such an effect on him? When just a week or two ago he'd been so sure no woman besides Milli ever could?

Maybe his mother was right about true love only striking once, but it seemed that true lust could come in many shapes and sizes.

Then Daisy tilted her chin up, looked him straight in the eye and said, 'So kiss me,' and he decided that wondering about that sort of thing could definitely wait for another day.

Right now, he had something much more important to do.

The wood of the door was still warm from the sun, a pleasant heat against her back—but nothing compared to the one between her and Jay. He was going to kiss her. And then he was going to make love to her. And that… Daisy couldn't quite decide if it was terrifying or glorious. Maybe both.

Either way, there was no chance in hell she was going to stop it now.

His mouth met hers and she sank into

the kiss, clutching at his arms to get closer, closer. This wasn't like any other first—or technically second—kiss in her experience. Those were drunken, fumbling, probing things. This kiss...

This kiss was something else. Jay's lips were confident and sure on hers, no hint of him being affected by the drinks they'd shared at the bar, although she could still taste the shots. His hands stroked up her side, her shoulder, just brushing against the curve of her breast rather than grabbing and groping her. And when she opened her eyes, he was staring right into them, so she could see the restraint in them. The desperate attempt to hold back from what he wanted.

What they *both* wanted.

'Okay?' he murmured against her lips.

Daisy shook her head, then grabbed him as he made to move away. 'More.'

That was all it took.

Jay fumbled with the handle until the door fell away behind them, and then they were inside, tripping over each other as they kissed their way to the bedroom, reluctant to let go for even a moment. Daisy stripped the shirt from his shoulders as he backed her towards the bed, popping the buttons from their holes in one swift movement to get her hands on the smooth skin of his shoulders and the muscles beneath. His chest was smattered with sandy hair, and she scratched her nails through it, working downwards to the buttons of his jeans.

The backs of her knees hit the bed frame—were they in her room or his? She hadn't been paying attention—and she sat abruptly, smiling as she realised she was now at exactly the right level to get those jeans off him. But Jay had other ideas. Raising her arms, he pulled her top up over her head, revealing the satin and lace half bra she'd chosen when planning the evening. With a small groan, he sank to his knees, taking one breast in his hand, the other in his mouth.

Well. Maybe she could live with him keeping the jeans on just a little longer, Daisy decided as he lowered her onto the bed, one knee on the mattress beside her as he covered her body with his and kissed his way down her body.

Just not *too* much longer.

Jay woke up the next morning to the strange sensation that he was being watched.

He tensed under the covers, eyes still tightly closed, until his brain caught up with his intuition.

Last night. The bar. Kissing Daisy against the door.

Daisy.

God, *Daisy.*

His mouth curved into a smile at the memory. Sex with Daisy had been every single bit as amazing as his imagination had told him it could be. From the moment they first kissed for real, her spiky, keep-out persona had dropped away, showing him the passionate woman underneath. Oh, she was still smart-mouthed and sarcastic, keeping him laughing even as he kissed every inch of her body. But there was a softer side, too. One that *wanted*. One that let him give.

And now she was watching him sleep. He loved that.

Smiling, he opened his eyes to wish her good morning—and found himself eyeball to eyeball with a goat.

Letting out a decidedly unmanly shriek, he jumped up to standing on the bed, a pillow clutched to his groin, as Genevieve chewed contently on the corner of the sheet.

'What the…?' Daisy swore sleepily, then sat up, brushing her dark hair out of her eyes. 'Jay? Oh. Good morning, Genevieve.'

'The builders fixed all the doors.' Jay sat cautiously back down on the mattress. 'How is she still even getting in?'

Daisy shrugged, the sheet falling away from her deliciously bare shoulders with the movement. 'Maybe she's a magic goat.'

He shot her a look, and she laughed.

'Okay, what will you give me to get rid of her?' she asked, wrapping the top sheet around her, toga style. It was too hot to sleep with any of the blankets—and they'd definitely kept each other warm the night before.

Jay raised an eyebrow. 'What would you like?'

Tilting her head slightly, Daisy pursed her lips, considering. 'Coffee.'

'Just coffee?'

'And pastries?'

'That's seriously all you want?' Perhaps last night hadn't been as good for her as it had for him, if she wasn't already desperate for a repeat performance. If it wasn't for the goat watching them, he'd definitely have been suggesting it by now.

Daisy nodded. 'Breakfast in bed. With you.' Her grin turned wicked, and his heartbeat kicked up a notch. 'After all, a girl needs sustenance to keep her stamina up.'

Jay grabbed his jeans from the floor and pulled them on. 'Deal. I'll make breakfast, you handle the goat, and we'll meet back here.' He leant in to kiss her swiftly on the lips—a kiss that turned rather more lingering as Daisy grabbed the back of his head and held him to her. Not that he was complaining.

'Breakfast,' he repeated, a little dazed, when they finally parted. 'Goat.'

'Then sex,' Daisy said, bouncing out of bed in her sheet toga. 'Definitely more sex.'

It was just as well that Matteo and Lorenzo had fixed the windows and the shutters, Jay mused the following night as he lounged in the shuttered cocoon of Daisy's bedroom. *Their* bedroom now, he supposed. He certainly hadn't been back to his for longer than it took to pick up a fresh box of condoms from his case.

'And what, exactly, made you think to pack those?' Daisy had asked, eyebrows arched where she'd sat in bed, as he'd returned with them.

'Nico put them in my case as a joke.'

Daisy had shaken her head. 'Knowing Nico, that was *not* a joke.'

'You're probably right.' He'd crawled back up the bed, tugging on her ankle to bring her flat on her back under him, knowing that it wouldn't take her long to kiss away his defences and flip them so she was on top. 'And you definitely weren't complaining when you found that strip of them in my jeans pockets after we made it back from the bar.'

'True. But I'm pretty sure Nico didn't put them there that night,' she'd pointed out.

Ah. Caught. 'Maybe I was just very, very hopeful. Or wishing very hard.'

'You're saying I make your wishes come true?'

He'd caught a bare nipple between his lips, and run his tongue around it, loving how she'd shivered under him. 'You make all my fantasies come true,' he'd murmured against her skin.

They'd had better things to do than talk after that.

In fact, after two whole days spent exclusively in bed with each other, they'd managed to not talk about anything of importance at all. Not what they were doing together, not the awards ceremony in Rome they had to leave for tomorrow, not the songs they were supposed to be writing… they'd just been lost in each other's bodies.

Not that he was complaining about that, either. But tomorrow morning there'd be a car, and a plane, then Rome, and other people. And at some point they really needed to talk about how this was going to work. Would they still be doing…this back in the real world?

'You look like you're thinking too hard,' Daisy murmured beside him. 'You should stop that. You might strain something.'

'I'm more worried about you breaking me than a little bit of thinking.'

'Worried you can't take the pace, old man?' Daisy's naked body slid over his in the dark, her mouth moving across his collarbone with light, butterfly kisses in a way she knew drove him crazy. 'Don't worry. You just lie back and let me take care of you.'

Then her kisses started to move lower, and Jay decided that maybe talking wasn't *that* important. They could discuss everything on the plane.

Right now, he just wanted to *feel*.

* * *

'Urgh, clothes.' Daisy threw her favourite short black dress back into her suitcase on top of a few other essentials, along with a pair of biker boots, and called it good. Just getting dressed felt like a challenge that morning. Not that she'd admit it to Jay—especially after her old man jokes—but her whole body ached, in a pleasurable way, from the last few days.

Nearly three days in bed with one man. She'd never done that before. Never *wanted* that before. And that was the part that made her nervous.

The idea had been that they'd get it out of their system, break the stupid tension, then carry on with their lives. Instead, she'd fallen into the best sex of her life, lost two full days and three nights in a haze of lust, and now she had to put on actual clothes and get on a plane to Rome.

Not ideal. Especially since they still hadn't talked about any of it, beyond their tipsy reasoning in the bar.

'The car's here. Are you ready?' Jay

asked from outside the bedroom door, and she tensed. Which was ridiculous. She'd literally laid herself bare for the man for the last three days. What on earth did she have to be nervous about now?

She took a breath and opened the door.

It was weird to see him in clothes again, she realised. To see him dressed like Jay Barwell, lead singer of Dept 135, not the guy she'd been living in a crumbling villa with for the last week or so. The man she'd been kissing and touching and making love with for the last seventy-two hours. He'd worn her out so thoroughly she'd even slept through his snoring.

Jay had also confessed, somewhere in the middle of all the sex, that some photo of them at the airport on their way out there had gone viral, and that, according to Kevin, the whole world knew they were off in some Italian love nest. Daisy was almost certain that Kevin had set up the photographer himself. And the worst part was, she couldn't even reasonably object any more, since it was technically accurate.

So now they were going back to the real world, where the public apparently believed they were a couple and their friends knew that they weren't, and she had no idea which one of those things was *actually* true.

Which meant they were going to have to Talk. With a capital T. About emotions and expectations and stuff—and Daisy *hated* those talks.

At least she already knew how this one would go. They'd agree that this was fun, and good, but they had to keep in mind that it was just for show. That he still loved Milli. That she didn't do relationships and love and all that anyway. She had too many dreams to chase.

As long as she still knew what it was that Jay wanted from her, she'd be okay. She just had to keep her eye on that. The transactional details of the affair, so to speak.

And not deck Nico when he figured out what was going on and started teasing her.

God, she really didn't want to go to Rome.

'I'm not sure we should leave Genevieve

alone,' she blurted out, earning herself an amused look from Jay.

'Really? The *goat* is the best excuse you can come up with? I was expecting at least something about leaving Matteo and Lorenzo unattended working on the villa, or how you hadn't paid them yet, or something.'

'Yeah, that would have been a better excuse,' Daisy admitted.

'As it happens, I've already spoken with Matteo. He and Lorenzo will keep working while we're away, and they have my number if any problems come up. I also insisted on transferring some money over for them for materials or what have you.'

Daisy froze. 'You shouldn't have done that. *I* should have done that. It's my villa.'

But Jay just shrugged. 'You can pay me back some time. It wasn't much, Daze. Just a couple of thousand.'

Pocket change to him, of course. But even now she knew, logically, she could afford it, Daisy's heart started to race at the idea of owing anyone that money. She fumbled for her phone, trying to open her banking app. 'I'll pay you now.'

'Save it for the plane, or we're going to be late.' He grabbed her suitcase and lifted it without obvious effort, but Daisy thought she saw a slight wince as he twisted, and realised she knew exactly which of last night's amusements had caused that muscle strain. 'Oh, and I asked Lorenzo to look after Genevieve, too,' he added, seemingly as an afterthought.

Daisy beamed. 'Thank you!'

'I knew you'd worry otherwise,' Jay said, with a soft smile. 'Now, come on, or we'll miss our flight.'

Maybe she was overthinking this. Maybe they could just carry on as before, now that all the sex was out of their system. Go back to being friends without ever having to discuss it.

Her hand brushed against his as she tried to reclaim her suitcase, and sparks sizzled up her arm as her body reacted to his touch—instinctive, automatic, and undeniable.

His gaze met hers and she knew he was feeling it too.

She swallowed. Hard.

'Car.'

'Right.'

'Now?'

'Yeah.' He stared a moment longer then shook his head. 'Now. Come on.'

The car bumped back down the hill towards reality. Daisy kept to her side of the back seat, staring out of the window, remembering all too well that this was where it had started. It wasn't that kiss onstage in Philadelphia that had kicked things off, not really. She'd been too certain that the kiss was just for show, so she'd been more annoyed than turned on.

But that moment when she'd fallen into his arms in the car up to the villa, when it was just the two of them and an oblivious driver. *That* was the first time she'd truly looked at Jay Barwell and thought, *Yes.*

Before that, she'd known he was gorgeous, but nothing more. After that…she'd had ideas.

And now? Now she knew *exactly* how he felt against her, inside her, and she wasn't likely to forget in a hurry. And given the sparks still between them, if they didn't want to give the driver a free—and probably very distracting—show they needed to keep their distance.

On the other side of the back seat, Jay appeared to be employing the same strategy, staring at his phone screen as if he cared what was on it and wasn't imagining dragging her back to bed again. Good. At least he couldn't distract her then. And he probably wouldn't notice her sneaking looks at him…

'Kevin sent me another email.'

Oh. Maybe he really *was* thinking of other things.

'What does it say?' Maybe the awards ceremony had been cancelled and they could go home.

Wait. *Home?*

Before she had a chance to analyse that thought further, Jay answered.

'Apparently there's a special live link-up planned from LA for the award I'm presenting, and Kevin wanted to give me a heads-up.'

Daisy frowned. 'Why would you care about that?'

'Because Milli is doing it, and they want me to do some scripted banter with her. Apparently we were both booked before we broke up, and now she's decided not to come to Italy but still needs to honour the contract, so...'

'Oh.' All the passion drained away from her as she realised how firmly back in the real world they were already. The world where Jay Barwell loved Milli Masters, and where she was just a fake distraction for the press.

At least she knew where she stood, and without even having to have that messy emotions conversation. That was a good thing.

Besides, it wasn't as if Jay's prowess in

the bedroom had made her fall in love with him or anything. He was a good friend and a great lay and a fun fake almost-fiancé. That was all.

She forced a smile as the cogs in her brain started turning. 'Then that means she'll be watching tonight. We should put on a show for her.'

Jay raised an eyebrow at her. 'A show?'

'Sure. I mean, we're going tonight as a couple, right? A *fake* couple, I mean,' she added hurriedly, in case he got the wrong idea. 'So we act up to it a bit. Should be even easier now—' She broke off.

'Now we've spent significant time together naked?' Jay finished for her.

'Basically, yeah.' If she was going to be his fake girlfriend, she was going to be the best one he ever had.

Jay looked out of the window for a long moment, before turning back to her. 'Okay. Say we were going to do that. What would it entail?'

Daisy grinned. Acting, that was all this was. Performing. And she'd been doing that for most of her life. As long as she didn't let messy emotions get involved, this should be easy.

'Well, for starters, I'm going to need a ring.'

CHAPTER EIGHT

JAY THREW HIS stuff onto the king-size bed of the hotel suite, then fell onto the mattress next to it, face first. He was exhausted. Never mind that his poor body had seen more exercise in the last three days than ever before—that, he could have coped with. Celebrated, even.

It was trawling around the jewellery shops of Rome that had finished him off.

He could hear Daisy pottering around the other bedroom of the suite, probably getting ready for the awards show. They should have had hours at the hotel to pre-pare, but their detour en route from the air-port to procure her an engagement ring had taken *much* longer than he'd expected.

'It doesn't have to be a real diamond or anything, but it does have to be big,' Daisy had said as they'd trawled the racks at the first jeweller's their incredibly patient driver had taken them to. 'We need to make sure it shows up on the cameras from the first moment we step out of the car. We want people talking about it before the awards show even starts.'

'And then we just smile coyly and look adoringly at each other, right?' He knew how this was played. He'd just never actually done it before—with Milli, he'd been so besotted he hadn't needed to act at all. But now, with the benefit of hindsight, he could see all her actions and behaviours for the performance they were.

'Could do.' Daisy had looked thoughtfully at the tray of rings in front of her. 'Or we could just play to our strengths. Coy has never particularly been one of mine.'

'Dare I ask what our strengths are?'

The look she'd given him had scorched him to the bone. 'If I need to tell you, then you really haven't been paying attention the last few days.'

Of course, after that he hadn't really been thinking about rings.

He had, thankfully, noticed the photographer trawling around behind them after the first couple of shops. He'd suspected the driver had tipped someone off. Probably Kevin, who'd tipped off the paparazzi. Perfect.

'Think it better had be a real diamond,' he'd murmured to Daisy as they'd leaned over the latest tray of jewels. 'We're being watched.'

She'd casually glanced over to where he'd indicated, then turned back to the shop-keeper. With one hand possessively placed on Jay's back, she'd pointed to the largest—and most expensive—ring in the tray. 'Let's try that one.'

Of course, it couldn't be quite *that* easy. They needed a ring that was the right size for her to wear to the awards ceremony that night, plus Jay suspected that Daisy had been enjoying leading the photographer a merry dance around Rome, so it had taken another three jewellery shops to find the perfect ring.

Well, perfect for the ruse, anyway. To Jay's mind it hung too big and heavy on Daisy's delicate fingers, clashing with her natural style. It was too sharp, too sparkly, too overwhelming to suit Daisy.

But he had to admit, it would definitely show up on the cameras tonight.

Kevin had cannily booked them a suite with two bedrooms, so they could stay together as far as the hotel and press were concerned but sleep separately. Still, after the last few days, Jay had assumed that they'd share a bedroom here as they had at the cottage. But as soon as they'd arrived, Daisy had taken her bags into the second bedroom and hadn't reappeared.

Jay wasn't quite sure what to make of that.

He'd meant to talk to her on the plane, to figure out exactly what this thing was between them, but instead the journey had been taken up with planning ways to level up their fake relationship. It would help, he supposed, if he knew what he wanted from this fling to start with.

Because it was a fling, right? That much he was pretty sure of.

Probably.

Yeah, he really needed to talk to Daisy.

But not before he'd had a proper, long, hot shower. The plumbing at the villa was still a bit hit and miss, and he'd been dreaming of a hotel bathroom for days. Of course, he'd also been imagining all the things he could do to Daisy in a shower like this...

Later. They'd get through tonight, then come back and enjoy all the benefits of this hotel suite. There'd be plenty of time to talk about what it all meant later, on the plane back, or once they were back at the villa, even. Yeah, that made sense. He'd wait until they had time and space alone again. Well, apart from the goat.

The shower went a long way to reviving him, and once he'd dressed in the suit the stylist Kevin had assigned them had sent up for him, he felt more or less ready to take on the real world again. At least fake-engagement-ring shopping with Daisy had taken his mind off the fact he was going to have to smile and play nice with Milli in front of hundreds of thousands of people across the globe tonight.

And even that was easier than seeing her in person, alone. Then, he knew, he wouldn't be able to stop himself asking her why. Why she'd let him believe that what they had could be real, when for her it was never more than a sham.

He wasn't sure he wanted to know the answer to that.

When they'd met, they'd both been rising stars. But it hadn't taken long for Milli's to eclipse his. From that point on he supposed it had been inevitable that she'd move onwards and upwards to something better.

But he wasn't thinking about Milli tonight. Not until he had to.

Opening the bedroom door, he headed into the suite's lounge, and found Daisy already there, dressed in a shimmering blue floor-length gown he'd never seen before. Cut high at the neckline, instead it plunged low at the back, baring her spine almost to the curve of her backside.

'Wow.'

'Yeah. Apparently now I'm your fake fiancée the stylist decided my wardrobe needed an upgrade.'

'It's gorgeous. *You're* gorgeous.' Her dark hair sat in waves against her head, angling down to her cheekbone on one side. She looked like a vintage film star, glamorous, beautiful, untouchable.

'It's not exactly my usual style,' Daisy admitted wryly. 'But I guess it goes with the ring.'

'It definitely does that.' His gaze darted to her left hand, and the huge rock sitting there, weighing her down. 'Think you'll be able to play guitar wearing that thing?'

Daisy shrugged, and the dress slid and shifted over her curves in a way that made him want to peel it right off her. 'Probably not. Maybe I'll need a stage ring too.'

'You're just in this for the jewellery, aren't you?' he joked as they heard a knock at the door.

'Because I'm such a magpie?' She patted his cheek and crossed the room to answer the door. 'I'll have you know I'm just in this for the hot sex.'

'More information than I needed.' Harry, standing behind the open door, looked between them, his gaze full of questions. Jay suspected he was going to have to answer at least some of them later tonight. More fun to look forward to. 'Glad to see you both made it,' Harry went on. 'If you're ready, the car's waiting downstairs.'

With a beaming, un-Daisy-like smile, his fake fiancée took his arm, ensuring that her left hand was in full view against his suit jacket. 'Then let's go!'

Daisy knew that the photos of her fake engagement ring would be on the Internet before they even reached the awards ceremony. There had definitely been ones of them ring shopping up online by the time they'd got back to the hotel. The media didn't mess around when it came to Jay Barwell's relationship status.

She just wished she understood it as well as the media seemed to think they did.

Harry had been shooting them both concerned glances since they'd left the hotel, while Kevin just looked blissful the whole time. Nico had elbowed Jay as they'd got into the car, making a joke about the condoms he'd slipped in his case. In response, Benji had rolled his eyes and pointed out that it was all just for show.

Daisy hadn't known how to tell them they were both right, so she hadn't said anything at all.

Jay was quiet too, probably thinking about the impending video chat with his ex. But as soon as they climbed out of the car onto the red carpet, he was all matinee-idol smiles for the cameras, holding her close against his side like a pretty accessory.

God, she hated this, she realised as the camera flashes blinded her. She hated being nothing more than an appendage to some man. She hated that people were more interested in her dress and her ring than her music. She hated that she was lying to the world, pretending to be something she'd never be.

The sort of woman Jay Barwell might marry.

How had it come to this? In some ways, events just seemed to have swept her up and dragged her along. But in others, she knew she'd chosen this. For Jay. To make him feel better.

Because however much she didn't want to talk emotions with him, she knew she had them. About him.

And that, she could already tell, was going to cause her nothing but problems.

'You okay?' Jay murmured softly as they waved goodbye to the press and the crowds and swept into the awards venue. 'You're clinging kind of tight there.'

'Not used to these shoes,' Daisy replied. Not a complete lie.

Just not the whole truth, either.

Basically exactly like their relationship.

The awards were being held in a theatre, newly refurbished inside, but classically styled on the outside. Daisy had to admire the Italian sense of style and she was glad that the stylist had provided her own outfit. Her usual favourite black dress and boots really wouldn't have fitted in here. The women were all so groomed and gorgeous, and the men in their suits all looked like James Bond, even if she knew that they were tattooed under their shirts and usually dressed in leather. Everyone seemed to have made a real effort tonight.

But it wasn't until she saw the signage over the stage that she realised *exactly* which awards ceremony Jay had brought her to tonight.

The Ascot Music Awards.

Ascot. Viv Ascot. How had she missed that?

Because Kevin had sent all the details to Jay, since he was the one appearing. She was just there as a hanger-on, of course. And naturally Jay had been far more obsessed with the details about Milli than linking it to her mysterious cottage acquisition.

'You didn't tell me it was the *Ascot* Music

Awards,' she muttered as they took their seats. Jay wasn't needed until much later in the ceremony, so had been told he'd be collected later to have his microphone set up and so on, and that he should just enjoy the show until then.

'The Ascot… Oh! I guess I didn't even register it. You think she might be here?'

Daisy shrugged. 'She was at the Ascot Music Festival in Copenhagen. Why not? And if she is, I want to ask her about the cottage.'

'About whether she knew what a state it was in? Or why she left it to you in the first place?'

'Both,' Daisy said darkly.

It was hard to concentrate on the actual awards being given out when all she wanted to do was scan the room for the woman she'd met and known only as Viv. She almost missed the moment when the staff came to get Jay to prepare to present his award, grabbing his hand at the last minute as he rose from his seat.

'You going to be okay?' she asked.

He didn't answer, exactly. Instead, he bent down and gave her a searing kiss. One that drove Viv Ascot, and the whole of Italy, from her mind for long seconds after he'd left to go backstage.

Nico leaned forward from his seat behind them. 'Okay, you've got to come clean with us. What's going on with you two?'

Harry pulled the drummer back. 'Ignore him. He only wants to know because he's got fifty quid riding on it in a bet with Benji.'

'True,' Benji put in.

'What's between you two is between you two,' Harry finished as the audience applauded the previous award winner.

'I'll let you know when I figure out what that is,' Daisy whispered to herself, her fingers still against her lips.

When he kissed her like that she wondered. She'd not had many long-term relationships in her life, and none lasting longer than a year. But even then, no other relationship had ever felt so passionate, so involved, in so little time.

Except that was just lust, wasn't it? It didn't mean anything more than that they had chemistry. And she'd known that from the first kiss he'd given her, onstage in Philadelphia, and that had *definitely* been just for show. Chemistry didn't mean anything.

Turning her attention back to the stage, Daisy sat bolt upright. There, just to one side, stood Viv Ascot, dressed in a gorgeous burgundy gown and flanked by a stern-looking security guy. She was talking to one of the other presenters, thanking her probably, Daisy assumed. It would be rude to interrupt.

But then it was pretty rude to leave someone a crumbling building without a single word of explanation, and Daisy had never been particularly polite, anyway. She was almost to her feet and edging her way out of the row towards Viv, when suddenly there was huge applause, and she realised that Jay had come onto the stage. How would it look if his doting fiancée abruptly skedaddled just when he was presenting his award?

Torn, she hovered on the edge of her seat,

trying to keep one eye on Viv and the other on the stage as the video link crackled to life and the perfect face of Milli Masters appeared on the screen.

'Hi there, Rome!' She waved, smiling wide enough to show off her perfect teeth, and Daisy tried not to hate her. She was the love of Jay's life.

Except she'd broken his heart. Maybe she was allowed to hate her a little bit.

'Great to see you, Milli,' Jay replied, obviously reading his lines from the autocue, since Daisy knew it wasn't actually great at all. 'And thanks for joining us all the way from LA.'

'Wouldn't miss it!' Milli replied, looking much happier about this whole arrangement than Jay was. Possibly because she was thousands of miles away.

Daisy tuned out for a second as she watched Viv embrace the woman she was talking to, then turn to leave. No! If she lost sight of her now she might never find her again in the crowd. Maybe if she just slipped out no one would notice…

206 ITALIAN ESCAPE WITH HER FAKE FIANCÉ

Suddenly, a bright light zeroed in on her eyeballs. She blinked, made sure she hadn't been abducted by aliens in the middle of a music awards ceremony, then smiled as she realised it was just the spotlight from the stage. Shining on her. For some reason she'd apparently missed.

'Looks like they noticed the rock on your left hand,' Harry whispered to her, so she must have looked pretty lost, too.

'So I hear congratulations are in order,' Milli was saying, although she didn't sound particularly celebratory. In fact, her smile was growing stiffer as she made her way through her lines, obviously read off a screen beside the camera. 'I'm just thrilled that you've found someone else—to sing duets with, I mean, of course.'

Forced laughter burst from the crowd, awkward in the face of Milli's obviously unhappy delivery, and Daisy tried not to sink back into her chair and disappear. Oh, God, this was awful. Milli's expression was thunderous, metres high on the TV screen for all to see. And Jay's was even worse, somehow—just completely blank. As if he couldn't even react to what was happening.

He pulled an envelope from his pocket. 'And the nominees are...'

Daisy looked to the side. Viv was gone. She'd missed her chance.

This whole evening was a total disaster.

'Should have stayed home with Genevieve,' she muttered to herself as Harry patted her shoulder.

'Well, that was horrible,' Jay said the moment they were through their hotel-room door and alone again. Dropping onto the sofa in the centre of the suite's main room, he waited for Daisy to join him.

She didn't.

He opened his eyes to find her still standing by the door, her high heels dangling from her fingers and the hem of the gorgeous shimmery blue gown pooling around her bare feet. 'You okay?'

'Yeah.' Crossing to the bar area, she ditched her shoes on the floor and pulled

out two glasses, then reached into the minibar. 'Drink?'

'Sure.' She poured two tiny bottles of liquor into the two glasses then handed him
one. Jay didn't even ask what it was before
downing it. 'I was ready for that.'

'It couldn't have been easy. Seeing Milli
again.' Daisy perched on the armchair opposite him, even though there was plenty
of space on the sofa.

Jay had to admit that didn't bode too well
for his hopes of getting her in his bedroom
tonight. Or his shower, for that matter.

No, apparently they had to have a discus-
sion about his disaster of a love life instead.
The perfect end to a horrible night.

'At least she was on the other side of an
ocean,' he said with a shrug. 'Seeing her in
person would be worse.'

'Because it hurts?'

'Because it makes me angrier.' Jumping
to his feet, he headed to the minibar for a
refill. This was clearly at least a two-drink
conversation.

Daisy was blinking at him in astonishment when he turned around. 'You? Angry? I don't think I've ever seen that.'

He huffed a slight laugh. 'I don't suppose you have. I…used to have a temper, as a kid—ask Harry. But I worked hard to control it. It takes a lot to make me lose my temper these days.'

He didn't mention that just dating Milli had been a sore test of that resolve. Or the fact that he'd only taken charge of it after breaking his brother's nose during an argument.

'But you were angry tonight?' Daisy pulled her feet up onto the chair, so just her bare toes poked out from under the hem of her dress. In so many ways, she looked just as she did back at the villa, when it was just the two of them and the goat.

Maybe that was why he answered her honestly.

'Yeah. I was bloody angry.'

'Because they scripted those awful lines about you "duetting" with me?'

Jay pulled a face. 'No. I mean, they were dreadful, but that's just bad writing. I guess someone spotted the ring on our way in and they shoehorned them in. There was supposed to be about another screen and a half of that "banter" between us but I just skipped them. I didn't want you to have to sit there through that with the spotlight on you.'

'Thanks.' Her voice was quiet, no mocking, no sarcasm.

He didn't like it.

Putting his glass down on the coffee table, he knelt down on the floor in front of her chair, his hands either side of hers. 'I was angry because it was all so fake. Her and me smiling and joking with each other when I still just want to yell "why?" at her whenever I see her face. She just walked out, then told me she'd gone in a social-media video shared with several million of our biggest fans and the whole world's media. I never got the chance to ask her why, to have that big argument that ends a relationship.'

Because for her, it hadn't been a relationship. It had been a marketing strategy.

But he couldn't admit that humiliation to Daisy—that he'd fallen in love, while she'd just been playing a part. Not tonight, anyway, not in this moment. But he realised to his surprise that he *did* want to tell her. To tell her everything, actually.

'The spotlight on me and the ring probably didn't help either, then,' Daisy said softly. 'I'm sorry about that. Maybe playing up to it all wasn't the best idea I've ever had.'

Jay shook his head. 'No, it was. I needed you there with me tonight.'

He looked up into her eyes and found an expression he'd not seen there before. He was used to seeing passion there now, wicked temptation. He'd seen humour and friendship and even blissful moments of creative synchronicity.

But tonight...was that pity? Or just concern?

Jay wasn't sure. But whatever it was, it drew him in.

'I'm glad I could help,' she said, voice quieter still.

He wanted to say more. There were questions he wanted to ask, things he wanted them to discuss, to clear up or decide between them. But right then he wanted something else more.

Rising up on his knees, Jay took her face between his hands and kissed her, gentle and long. And somehow, it felt completely different from every time he'd kissed her over the last few days.

It wasn't that the passion had changed—he could still feel it, simmering beneath the fancy clothes and the exhaustion. But for the first time, that wasn't all their kiss was about. He wasn't touching her to drag her back into bed, to find their mutual pleasure again.

He was kissing her because he was thankful she was in his life. Because she was the one thing that felt real in his crazy fake world right now.

Except, in reality, she was the fakest part of it.

He pulled back, his gaze drawn to the

sparkle of her pretend engagement ring in the lamplight.

At least this time he knew that this wasn't real, however it felt in the moment.

At least discovering the truth couldn't tear his heart out again this time.

'Come to bed with me tonight?' he asked, his words barely a whisper, but she heard them.

'Yes,' she answered. And for a moment, Jay could almost believe he'd asked her another question altogether.

CHAPTER NINE

DAISY HAD NEVER been so grateful to see anywhere as her little cottage on the cliff.

'Genevieve!' she called out as she jumped out of the car. The little goat came trotting over from where she was eating a patch of prickly-looking plants.

Behind her, she saw Jay grabbing their bags and thanking the driver, but she just hugged her goat and gave thanks that she was home.

Home. That was what this place was. Which was crazy, since she'd spent less than two full weeks there in her whole life. But it was *hers* in a way that nowhere else in the world ever had been.

Maybe she didn't need to ask Viv why after all. All she'd really needed was to spend some time away from the place back in the real world, and she'd learned to appreciate the value it held. Far greater than a new job or a trip around the world, for her.

This place was her sanctuary. Her escape. And she had a feeling she was going to need it in the weeks and months to come.

She and Jay still hadn't talked about what was happening between them. After his confession about how he felt seeing Milli again, it just hadn't been the time. He'd said he was angry, but Daisy suspected that was just man-talk for upset and heartbroken.

He'd made love to her that night as if it was the last time, and she'd braced herself for him telling her this morning that he wasn't coming back with her. That he was heading to LA to talk to Milli properly at last.

But he hadn't.

Matteo and Lorenzo appeared from around the side of the villa and excitedly pointed out new improvements to them both, some that they'd finished before they'd left for Rome, but some that were utterly unexpected and new. Daisy sus-

pected they must have had some help over
the last couple of days to get it all done.
Outside, the finished roof, the windows and
the painted front door all finally looked like
the photo the solicitor had shown her of the
cottage in better days. And inside, all the
stained and grubby walls had been painted
a fresh, bright white. The floors and bath-
rooms had been cleaned, and even the dated
furniture didn't look so awful against a nice
backdrop.

'It's amazing. Thank you!' She threw her
arms around each of the men in turn. 'How
much do I owe you?'

'We've already been paid,' Matteo replied, looking at Jay. 'But if you need anything else doing, just call us.'

'How much do I owe *you*, then?' she
asked, turning to Jay as the builders returned to packing up their stuff.

Jay shrugged. 'Call it a housewarming
gift.'

'You can't just fix up my house as a gift.'
Gifts were flowers from the service station,
or knock-off perfume. And yeah, okay, Jay

could afford many times the sort of gifts her old boyfriends used to give her. But this was her *house*. It was personal.

'You let me stay here.' Jay stepped closer, his hands at her waist, his forehead close to hers. 'You helped me find my music again. You got me drunk and made me relax. You gave me the most fun and passionate three days of my entire life. And then you put on a stupid ring you hate and pretended to be in love with me so that I wouldn't be humiliated in front of my ex and the whole world in Rome. I think I can pay for some roof tiles.'

'Well, when you put it like that…' She kissed him. 'Thank you.'

'Thank *you*. I honestly don't know how I'd have made it through last night without you.'

He'd already made his thank-yous for that in bed the night before, as far as Daisy was concerned. And now it was over, she didn't want to dwell on it.

Especially because it made her start thinking about how heavy the ring on her left hand felt—more from the lies than the diamond.

They dumped their bags and wandered down the hill into the village for lunch, pulling up chairs at the café Daisy had discovered on their first day and ordering crispy, thin pizzas loaded with fresh vegetables and deli meat.

'You realise at some point we're going to have to fake break up.' Daisy bit into her pizza and moaned at how good it tasted. Swallowing, she carried on. 'I mean, unless you want to actually fake marry me and fake divorce me later.'

Actually, that didn't sound so terrible. They could just keep hanging out, writing songs, having sex and laughing together until one of them met someone they *actually* loved—that would be Jay, she was certain—and decided it was time to move on.

Okay, *then* it would probably suck a lot. Because she'd have grown used to having him around by then. To the life they had together.

'You'd have to give me a damn good divorce settlement, though,' she said, because she couldn't say, 'I'll miss you when this is over.' That wasn't the deal they'd struck.

Jay pulled a face. 'Maybe you'd have to give *me* one. You might be the one who becomes an amazingly huge star and decides I'm not big enough for you any more.'

There was something in his voice. A hint of bitterness, maybe.

'Is that what you think happened with Milli?'

He shrugged and stared down at his pizza. 'How would I know? She never talked to me directly, remember? But from what I learned later…' He paused, as if saying the words was the hardest thing he'd ever do. 'Yes. She left me when I couldn't do anything more to add to her reputation or celebrity. Because while I thought we were in love, for her it was publicity, like it is with you and me. Only difference is, we both know what the score is this time.'

Daisy's heart hurt for him. He'd been in

love and Milli had been faking it all along. God, that had to screw a person up, right?

'We definitely do.' Daisy forced herself not to look at his engagement ring on her finger. Not to imagine for even one second that this relationship was something other than it was.

Even though she was afraid she was starting to want it to be, with every moment they spent together.

Which was why she had to focus on how this was all going to end. She didn't want to end up broken as Jay had been by Milli. She didn't even have the excuse of not knowing that it was all for show from the outset.

'You know, my mum would be completely baffled by this conversation,' Jay said, a fond smile on his face.

'You said once that she didn't understand all this fake relationship stuff? I mean, if anyone actually does.'

'Yeah. She and my dad…they were the real thing. So in love they could never even look at another person.' A shadow fell across his face for a second. 'Until he died.'

'I'm sorry,' Daisy blurted automatically.

Jay shook his head. 'It was a long time ago now, when I was a teenager. Afterwards… I threw myself into music as a sort of coping mechanism, you know?'

'I know,' Daisy said, with feeling. 'When I was younger, growing up in Liverpool, music was my only escape. Practising, getting better, it was a distraction from everything that was awful at home or at school. And I knew, even then, that it was going to be my way out—the one thing that would help me escape the place I grew up and the family that didn't want me. The same way my mum did.'

She pulled back as Jay reached out to take her hand. She hadn't meant to say so much—far more than she'd shared with anyone else since she'd left Liverpool.

'Your mum was a musician?' Jay asked softly.

'A wannabe one,' Daisy said with a shrug. 'She left when I was six to chase fame. But since nobody has ever heard of her since, I'm guessing it didn't go so well. She left me her mandolin, though, so I guess I have her to thank for my career.'

Jay's gaze was soft, sympathetic, but he didn't push her any more on the subject. He had to know her well enough to understand that she'd already said far more than she was really comfortable with.

'My dad taught Harry and me to play guitar. That's why we started the band together, after he died. Sort of in his memory.'

'I bet he'd have loved that. I'm sure your mum did too.'

'Yeah.' His smile faltered a little. 'It kept him alive for us all, I guess. Mum…she's always said that there's only one true love for a person—a soul mate. Dad was hers. She was only in her forties when he died, but she's never even gone on a date since.'

Daisy tried to imagine a love that deep and couldn't. She'd never seen it. But Jay obviously had. No wonder discovering that Milli was faking it had hurt him so badly—he'd been expecting the real thing, like his parents had.

She wanted to say something sympathetic. Something to show she understood him, felt for him, wanted to be there for him.

But she was still Daisy Mulligan, however much he was messing with her emotions. So instead she said, 'Huh. Given how much sex *you've* had since the love of your life walked out, I'm guessing this is one of those things that's different for guys?'

That surprised a laugh from him, at least. 'Only with you,' he said.

His words caught her in the chest, and she fought to keep her light-hearted, careless composure. 'Okay, then, back to the point at hand. How are we going to do it?' she carried on, forcing a smile. 'Break up, I mean. Milli already stole "dumping you on social media," so we need something new, right? Do you want to dump me this time? Or shall I catch you with another woman? Or hire a skywriter?'

Finally, Jay laughed at her last suggestion. 'This is clearly going to take some thought,' he said. 'I think we'll need to order pudding, too. I bet this place does a great tiramisu.'

'Works for me,' Daisy said, with a smile she couldn't quite feel.

If all she could have with Jay was a few months of a fake relationship, at least she could make sure they both had as much fun with it as possible.

Lunch lingered long into the afternoon, with liqueur coffees to follow the pudding, and their break-up suggestions becoming more outrageous by the minute. By the time they staggered back up the hill to the villa, arms around each other and pausing to kiss at regular intervals, they'd reached 'fighting over custody of Genevieve' in their break-up plans and scripted some hilarious pleas to 'think of the goat!' for the other band members to put out on social media.

Jay couldn't imagine ever laughing so much with Milli, even if he *had* known what the deal was between them.

He swung Daisy around by her hand until she toppled into his arms, and held her close. 'We don't have to do any of this yet though, right? The breaking up, I mean?'

She smiled up at him, but there was something brittle behind that smile. Something at odds with her words. 'Of course not. Not while we're still having fun.'

He bent his head so his lips grazed hers. 'I'm still having a lot of fun.'

'So am I,' she murmured back. 'Want to go have more fun back at the cottage?'

'Definitely.' They raced the rest of the way along the cliff hand in hand, and Jay felt his heart and his spirits rising and rising—

Until he saw the car parked outside Daisy's cottage.

Daisy skidded to a halt beside him. 'Is that—?' She broke off, as Kevin stepped out of the car, raising his sunglasses to look at the building.

'Nice place.' Kevin turned to them and lowered his sunglasses again. 'We thought we'd stop by and hear what you guys have been working on.'

Which, of course, was when the car doors opened and the rest of the band tumbled out.

'Do we even have enough bedrooms for them all?' Daisy hissed to Jay after she dragged him into the bathroom, while outside the locked door Kevin, Harry, Nico and Benji made themselves at home in her cottage's living area.

'As long as I share with you we have,' Jay said. 'And I think I saw some more bed linen in one of the cupboards. Food, however…'

She pulled a face. 'We'll have to go shopping again. Did they tell you they were coming?'

'Not a hint.' And he intended to have very strong words with his brother about that shortly.

'They want to hear the songs we've been working on.' Daisy chewed her lip nervously, and Jay fought not to kiss away her concerns. 'Except we've not exactly been working hard the whole time…'

'I think we worked damn hard, thank

you.' He pulled her into his arms again and wished, with all his heart, that it were just the two of them again. And Genevieve, of course. 'Just not on the music.'

'Which is the part they've come to hear. Keep up.'

He kissed her, just because he could. 'Stop worrying. We have two songs.'

'One we hate.'

'And one that will knock their socks off. And that will buy us enough leeway with them to get us time to write the rest.'

She still looked uncertain, but she nodded, all the same. 'Fine. But I'm not playing hostess or anything. Nobody in there actually believes I'm your doting fiancée. They're *your* band, you look after them.'

'Noted. But if you go pour them all drinks, I'll make up the beds for everyone.'

'Done.' She pressed a swift kiss to his cheek. 'But I'm hiding the limoncello in our bedroom.'

'Good plan.'

He gave her a moment to escape to the drinks cabinet they'd stocked up over the last couple of weeks, then slipped out to find the bed linen.

But Harry was waiting for him in what used to be his bedroom.

'Kevin wanted to come on his own, but I thought you might need backup,' he said, before Jay could ask. 'Also, I have questions. Well, one question.'

Jay shook out a pillowcase. 'Which is?'

'What the hell are you doing?'

'Making up the beds.'

'That's not what I meant.'

'I know.' Jay sighed. Of all of the band, his family and friends, Harry knew most how badly he'd been broken by Milli, and the method of her departure. But he'd never told Harry the worst of it. That it wasn't the public humiliation—well, it wasn't *just* that. It was that the love he'd imagined, the future he'd believed in…none of it had even been real to begin with.

But Harry…he wasn't just his friend or his band mate. He was his brother. And he worried, Jay knew, the same way he worried about Harry.

'Look, it's okay. With Milli… I thought I was in love. I thought I knew what I was doing. But it turned out that it was all just a publicity stunt to her. That our relationship meant nothing more than the next headline.'

Harry winced. 'I… I wondered. Because of the way she ended it. And that weird thank-you message from her publicist afterwards.'

'Yeah. That was the real giveaway.'

Jay—thanks for the memories—and the headlines! Milli

If he hadn't already suspected the truth, that would have sealed it.

'On the plus side, at least you can tell Mum that Milli definitely *wasn't* your one true love?' Harry suggested.

Jay chuckled. 'Yeah. I can definitely do that. I mean, how could I be in love with someone who didn't even really exist? Milli, she was just a character, a facade. I see that now.' Because Daisy, even when she was faking being in love with him, was anything but. She was *real*. Even if the game they were playing with the media wasn't.

'So you're not mooning over Milli any more,' Harry concluded. 'That's good. I just don't want to see you getting hurt again.'

Jay shook his head. 'It's different with Daisy…it's not like with Milli. This time, we *both* know what we're doing—we're playing a part, acting at being in love for our fans because it sells records. Nobody is going to get hurt this time.' It was probably a bad thing that he didn't even sound convincing to his own ears.

Because he knew, already, that it would be all too easy to get used to having Daisy around. Spending time with her. Listening to her laugh. Making love to her at night and waking up to her in the mornings.

Daisy was prickly and sarcastic and short-tempered and basically the opposite of the easy-going, relaxed life and personality he'd worked hard to develop for himself. And she was definitely the polar opposite of Milli's sugary sweetness.

He liked all that about her. He liked most things about her.

That was the problem.

'We were just talking today about how we're going to stage our break-up,' Jay went on, not entirely sure if he was trying to convince Harry or himself.

'Why?'

'Because it was funny?' It had been, somehow. Hilarious even, at the time. But thinking about it now gave him chills.

'I mean, why are you planning on breaking up? Did you check your social-media notifications today?' Jay shook his head, and Harry pulled out his phone. 'Then you might not have seen this.'

Holding up the screen so Jay could see it clearly, Harry gave him a knowing look. Jay ignored him and focussed on the photo on the phone.

It was him and Daisy in Rome, of course. But not any of the staged photo opportunities they'd manufactured that night at the awards ceremony. It wasn't a shot of them on the red carpet, or his kissing her ostentatiously in front of the cameras. It was the smaller, quieter moment after it was all over, when she'd taken him aside to check he was okay after Milli, and then told him about seeing Viv and not being able to talk to her.

In the shot, their heads were bent close together, and he had one hand at her waist, while she pressed her palm against his cheek. She looked about to reach up and kiss him—and from his memory, she had.

But most of all, they looked like a couple. A real couple.

A couple in love.

He pushed the phone away. 'Apparently we both have a future in the movies if we want it. Now, if you'll excuse me, I have to make up the beds for our impromptu guests.'

He couldn't start believing there was anything more to this relationship than a good publicity opportunity. Jay didn't want to dwell on possibilities that could only break his heart again. Not when he was only just recovering from the last time.

Harry would have to understand that.

Daisy had been looking forward to waking up to the silence of the villa on the cliff top again, after the busyness of Rome. But instead, she woke the next morning to a headache, an empty bed, and someone shouting about a goat.

'Calm down, Nico,' she heard Jay saying, out in the hallway. 'It's only Genevieve.'

She grinned to herself. At least her gatecrashing guests weren't getting everything their own way. Genevieve was clearly staking her claim to the place, too.

Snuggling back down under the duvet, Daisy grabbed her phone from the nightstand. Jay would probably see the goat back outside, then hopefully come back to bed again. Maybe she'd pretend to be asleep, so he could wake her up properly…

But while she waited, she might as well check in on her notifications.

She scrolled straight past too many re-posts of yesterday's star photo—the one of her and Jay in Rome looking a little too loved up for her comfort—to see if there was anything new to report. And stopped as soon as she saw Milli Masters' sugary-sweet smile in her feed.

Why was Milli talking about her?

Apprehension pressing on her chest, she clicked the link.

Jay and Daisy love-fest a fake, claims ex.

Milli says, 'Jay and I are soul mates, even if we can't be together right now.'

Oh, hell.

A message notification pinged—Aubrey.

Anything you want to tell us?

The message was linked to the photo of Daisy and Jay.

She sent one back.

It's a long story. Can I fill you in later? I kind of need to talk to Jay right now.

Aubrey sent back a reply immediately.

I bet you do. And don't worry—looks like Jessica has a 'long story' for us too. I just hope my summer adventures are half as exciting as you two have been having!

Daisy pulled a face at the phone screen. She wasn't sure she'd class this as 'exciting'. More probably a terrible mistake.

She clicked back to the story about Milli. It didn't get any better on full reading.

Anger surged up inside her. This woman had led Jay on, dumped him on social media, broken his heart—and now she had the audacity to come trampling over their relationship? Yes, technically she was right—it *was* fake. But what if it weren't? What if Jay really had found happiness again? Then she'd be purposely trying to ruin it.

Witch.

Had he seen it yet? Was that why he'd already been out of bed when Nico started yelling about Genevieve?

Suddenly, Daisy's lazy morning in bed wasn't looking so likely.

The bedroom door opened and Jay slipped in.

'You look tired,' she blurted without thinking.

'Just what every guy wants to hear.' He ran a hand through his hair. 'I couldn't sleep last night. I was thinking about—'

'Milli,' she finished for him.

He gave her a curious look. 'That third song we couldn't get right, actually. I think I've got an idea that might fix it.'

He was focussing on the music. That was a good thing. She should encourage that. 'Want me to grab my guitar? We might have to work on it in here though, if we want anything approaching privacy.'

'Good idea. I gave Harry a shopping list and encouraged him to take the others down to the village with him when he went foraging, by the way.'

'An even better idea. Wait here.'

Daisy crept out into the living area, hanging back until she heard the front door close behind Harry and the others, grabbed her guitar and ran back to the bedroom. Maybe they didn't *have* to hide in there with the others gone, but she liked the more intimate vibe it gave their work. Plus it meant they wouldn't be interrupted when the others returned.

'Okay.' Settling cross-legged on the bed, she pulled her guitar into her lap and tightened up the tuning. 'Tell me what you were thinking.'

This part was so easy, she realised as he started talking—a flow of thoughts on the tone of the song, the way the words and harmonies twined around each other. Here, in the music, was where they understood each other best. Music and sex, that was what they had.

And as she listened to him, as he took her guitar from her hands and played her what he meant, then handed it back so she could repeat it back, with her own flair and additions, she wished they could stay in this bubble for ever.

Just the two of them, the music, and the

goat. Here in the middle of nowhere, forgetting about the rest of the world.

Time passed differently when they were lost in the music; Daisy had noticed that before. Still, when the knock on the door came, she was startled out of her concentration.

'Must be Harry back with the shopping,' she said, stretching her arms over her head to work out the kinks in her back—and enjoying the way Jay's gaze hovered around her breasts as she did so. 'How long do you think it'll take them to realise that the door's not locked?'

'If the damn goat can get in here unaided, I'm sure my brother can manage it,' Jay answered, still watching her stretch. 'Do you think this one is ready for Kevin yet?'

Daisy waggled her head from side to side. 'Maybe. It's definitely miles better than it was last week. I can't help but think it's still missing something, though. A last stanza, maybe. It feels…unbalanced.'

Jay shrugged. 'It'll come.'

There was more hammering on the door,

and Daisy rolled her eyes before sliding off the bed and heading for the door. 'Harry, you're officially dumber than a goat,' she yelled as she made her way through the living room. At least living in the middle of nowhere meant she didn't have to worry about answering the door in the boy shorts she slept in and Jay's T-shirt she'd pulled on after rolling out of bed. The boys had all seen her in worse on the tour bus; privacy wasn't really a thing for them on tour, and they'd just included her as one of the boys from the start.

'You'd better have brought my limoncello,' she griped as she opened the door—

And stopped.

Because Harry wasn't there. Nor was Kevin or Nico or Benji or even Matteo or Lorenzo or Geraldine.

Standing on her doorstep, one perfectly manicured hand raised to knock again, was Milli Masters.

With half the world's media waiting behind her.

CHAPTER TEN

'JAY! IT'S FOR YOU!'

It was the strain in Daisy's voice that made him jump from the bed and race through the cottage. But even then, he didn't expect to see his ex-girlfriend standing in the Italian sunshine on the cliff top outside Daisy's home.

Daisy stood aside the moment he arrived on the scene. 'This is way above my pay grade,' she muttered as she brushed past him, back to her bedroom.

Their bedroom.

He heard her shut the door behind her, and a horrible sense of foreboding flooded through him as he realised it might not be *their* bedroom any more. This whole charade might be about to crash to a close.

And he couldn't do anything about it, because he had to deal with Milli and her media circus.

'What are you doing here?' he asked in a sharp whisper as he angled himself out of the front door and shut it behind him. He wasn't inviting Milli inside. This was Daisy's place—their place, even—and Milli had no right to be there. Kevin and Harry and the others were one thing, as was Genevieve. But Milli was definitely less welcome than even the bloody goat.

Milli's large grey eyes widened innocently. He didn't believe a millimetre of it. Whatever had brought her here, he knew for a fact that she'd have a plan.

'Aren't you pleased to see me? I just flew in from LA. After I saw you onstage in Rome... I just *had* to come, Jay. You can see that, can't you?'

Was she really talking to him, or to the reporters behind her? Because while he'd kept his voice low, Milli was projecting to the seagulls on the roof.

'No, I can't see that. So I'll ask you again. What, *exactly*, are you doing here, in Italy, and my fiancée's house?' It was amazing how easily that flowed from his mouth. Fiancée. Daisy. Strange how right it felt, when he knew full well it was a lie.

Milli didn't look convinced, though. Some of the studied innocence fell away as her expression hardened, and she dropped her voice a little. 'Oh, come on, Jay. Nobody *really* believes you're going to marry that groupie of yours.'

'Daisy is *not* a groupie.' Was he snarling? He might actually be snarling. God, the media must be loving this.

Time to pull it back. What would that media-training woman Kevin sent him to see say? What about the counsellor after he broke Harry's nose as a kid? Probably both the same thing.

Deep breaths. Only you are in control of your body, your emotions. Don't give that power away.

He knew this. He'd worked hard at this.

Stare between her eyebrows so you're not looking her in the eye but it looks *as if you are. Smile, even if you don't want to. Keep your voice even. Don't let her know that she's getting to you.*

That was all media training. How to fake being a celebrity, rather than a human being with feelings. That was what he was now, right? It was what Milli had wanted him to be, what Daisy wanted. What his fans wanted, even.

It went with the job.

He still wasn't inviting Milli inside, though. And actually, he kind of thought she didn't want to go in, anyway. How would the press report on her every anguished facial expression if they couldn't see her?

Right now, she shot him a warning look, then settled her expression back into earnest innocence. Her words, however, muttered too low for anyone else to hear, were anything but.

'Come on, Jay, you know the game. We've had the dramatic break-up, now it's time for the reconciliation. It'll hit all the papers, boost record sales for the quarter, get us plenty of free publicity. We can probably start looking at rings and wedding venues if that's what you really want—I agree, it's definitely an attention winner, and if we go the "conscious-uncoupling" route in a few years we can probably both retain our images through the divorce.'

'You dumped me. On social media.' His insides felt as if they were falling through the porch steps. He'd known—he'd *known* that this was all just part of the show for her. But she'd never admitted it so clearly before. All those months wasted, thinking he actually mattered to her as more than a publicity prop.

Not a mistake he ever intended to make again.

Milli rolled her eyes. 'Because it was *time*. People don't stay interested in happy couples. They want the drama, the *will they-won't they*. So I gave them that. I didn't expect you to run off and start another fake relationship with the first girl who crossed your path—let alone take her rock shopping. Kevin must have been really worried about your tour figures to push you into that.'

Jay ignored the part about Kevin. 'I thought you were gone. For good.' He didn't bother arguing against the 'fake relationship' accusation. She was right. And, even if she wasn't, she'd never believe it anyway.

'That's because you never paid any attention to everything I was doing to build our profile as a celebrity couple!'

'Because I thought we were an *actual* couple! In love!' Shame burned through him as he admitted it. How much he'd fallen for her charms, for what he'd believed they could have together. He'd thought they'd be like his parents, still in love after forty years of marriage.

How wrong could he have been?

The look Milli gave him was almost pitying.

'Come on, Jay. Really? I knew you were naive, but not even you could have believed that.'

He didn't answer. What else was there to say?

Over her shoulder, he spotted a small commotion at the back of the press pack—

Harry, Kevin and the others returning from their jaunt into town. Excellent. Just what this situation needed—more people who thought they had a say in his romantic life.

Where was Daisy? He wanted her beside him, to show Milli how little he needed her now. How he'd found something better—more meaningful, more intense. He and Daisy were friends, they laughed together, they made music together.

But she wasn't there, of course. Because everything he had with her was just as fake as what he'd had with Milli. The only difference was that Daisy had been upfront about that from the start.

Milli glanced back over her shoulder too. He wondered if she saw the thunderous expression on Harry's face. Maybe *that* was why she said what she did next.

'Jay, there's only one reason I've come to Italy.'

Her voice carried out over the cliffs. He wondered if Daisy could hear it inside. If she couldn't, he was sure the video would be on social media for her to watch within moments.

'To win you back. We're soul mates, you and I. And I can't lose you to someone unworthy of your love. Come back to me, my love. We're endgame. Meant to be. And I'm not leaving Italy until you admit it. You know how to find me when you're ready.'

Then, with a swift kiss to his lips, she descended the steps like a princess, climbed back into the car that had brought her, and was driven away down the hill, followed by the scrambling media as they tried to keep up and file copy at the same time.

Leaving just his manager, his brother and his band mates staring at him.

And Jay with no idea what to do next.

Daisy heard the front door open again and people talking over each other as they came inside her house. Her home.

She couldn't hear Milli's voice amongst them, thankfully, but from what she'd been able to overhear through her open window, the pop star had left the ball thoroughly in Jay's court.

She wanted him back. Of course she did. Daisy knew the type perfectly—never more interested in a guy than when someone else had him. Jay had been getting more publicity over his fake romance with Daisy than he had for months before his break-up with Milli. Of course Milli wanted in on that.

And Jay, bless him, would fall for it too. Because he loved her, even though he knew she only loved his fame. More evidence, if Daisy needed it, that love was a ridiculous, hurtful thing.

There's always a price. Would Jay pay it?

There was a soft knock on her door. 'Daisy? Kevin wants us all out here, if that's okay.' Harry's voice, not Jay's, apologetic but firm. Daisy knew it didn't matter if it was 'okay' or not, whatever Harry said. This was part of the job.

Her *heart* was part of the job, now.

She dragged herself off the bed and into the living room, where the others were all ranged around the chairs and perched on the coffee table. She leant against the door frame, outside the group—she wasn't a band member, she wasn't management, and she definitely wasn't actually Jay's fiancée. She had no place here, for all that it was her house.

Jay sat in the armchair, hands folded in his lap, his head bent as he stared at the floor. Daisy willed him to look up, to meet her gaze, to show her what he was feeling, but he didn't.

Kevin was holding court, pacing in front of the window. 'This is actually great news! I mean, Daisy, you've been a real sport and all, but now we can call an end to this fake engagement thing and Jay can get back with Milli! She's a bigger star anyway—no offence, Daisy,' he added, with a brief glance in her direction.

'It's the best of both worlds, mate,' Nico agreed. 'We all still get to tour with Daisy, and you get to sleep with Milli Masters. Living the dream, Jay.' He held one hand up for a high five, which Jay ignored, so he turned to Benji to get one instead.

'Sounds more like a nightmare to me,' Harry objected quietly. 'Jay, you can't let her get to you again. Not when you have the chance at something more. *Think* about this, please. Think about Mum—and Dad. I know you. You've always wanted what they had together. The real thing. You'll never be happy in a fake relationship.'

But Jay stayed silent. Daisy tried to read his face, what little of it she could see from the shadows of the angle he sat at, but there was nothing there. He'd closed off again, completely, the way he'd been when Milli first left.

Harry was right, Daisy knew. Jay wouldn't be happy with Milli, not for ever. He wanted what his parents had, and that wasn't on offer there. But she knew from watching her friends settle for less than their dreams, all because of love, that there was no telling a person in love anything logical. They just couldn't hear it. They had to discover it on their own, as her mother had—eventually, and probably too late.

Kevin obviously took Jay's silence as

agreement with his plan. Had Jay ever argued back with him? she wondered. Or was he so focussed on staying calm and being Zen that he forgot to even fight for what mattered to him?

He sure as hell wasn't going to fight for her, she could see that.

'Okay, so what we need to do now is figure out the best way to break you two up—what line to take, so Jay can go back to Milli without there being any backlash,' Kevin said.

'Heaven forbid we fight over custody of the goat,' she murmured—and Jay looked up for the first time and met her gaze.

She wished she could read what was going on behind those troubled green eyes of his, but she couldn't. She had no idea what he was thinking at all.

She just knew that suddenly all the things they'd been joking about yesterday—elaborate break-up schemes, who got Genevieve in the separation—none of them seemed the slightest bit funny any more.

'Stop,' Jay said, from nowhere, still staring at her. 'I need to talk to Daisy.'

She blinked, but nodded, and took his hand as he stood and led her, not to the bedroom as she'd expected, but straight out the front door to the cliff edge where they'd sat and talked music. Where she'd told him she didn't want him to propose to her.

How much had changed since then.

'What do I do, Daze?' he asked, raking his fingers through his hair as he looked at her. 'Tell me what I should do.'

Don't go back to her. Marry me instead.

The thought bubbled up in her totally unbidden, and she only just caught the words before they flew out of her mouth.

That was crazy thinking. She couldn't—wouldn't—marry Jay. They had a fake relationship, that was all. They weren't in love with each other or anything stupid like that.

Except…except her heart hurt to think of him leaving. Every muscle in her body wanted to grab him and make him stay here, at the cottage with her and Genevieve, for ever. She wanted to wake up to him in the mornings, make love to him before she fell asleep. She wanted to laugh at ridiculous jokes with him and write countless songs with him and go out for pizza and coffee and laugh at his attempts at Italian.

She wanted him. For her own.

For ever.

Oh, God, she was in love with Jay Barwell. How *stupid* could she get?

She'd let a fake romance feel real, and now look where she was. About to get her heart broken, just as she'd sworn she never would again.

She knew what love did to people. It made them give up their dreams. Would her mum have been a success if she hadn't married her father? Daisy couldn't know for sure.

But she knew that Jay wanted forever and everything, the way his parents had loved. And she wasn't that, for him. She was a pretend fiancée to boost ticket sales.

Which was why she couldn't let him know how she felt. They had passion and they had friendship, but he'd never even hinted at anything more between them. If she wanted to keep at least the friendship, and the music, and her career, and her heart vaguely intact, then she had to make sure Jay never knew how she felt.

Swallowing hard, Daisy put on her best mask, and prepared to lie.

'Kevin's right,' Daisy said. 'Milli would be better for your career than me. You should get back together with her. I mean, you know we'll come up with a great break-up, right?'

The words hit him harder than he'd expected. There were no surprises in them, nothing he didn't already know. They'd been joking about their break-up plan just yesterday, after all.

But somehow, it hadn't felt really real then.

It did now. And somehow it hurt, far, far more than he'd thought it would.

'You…you want me to get back together with Milli?' He had to be sure.

Daisy gave a nonchalant shrug. 'Sure. I

mean, if it keeps the label happy. One fake relationship is much like another, right?'

But they weren't, he realised. Not at all.

He'd assumed the difference between his two relationships was that he'd believed in true love with Milli but known the score with Daisy from the start. He'd thought it was more fun, more real with Daisy because he *knew* it wasn't.

But that wasn't it at all.

His fake relationship with Daisy felt more real than anything before in his life. Because it was *Daisy.*

Because she felt music the way he felt music. Because his skin fizzled when she touched him, and because she came alive under his fingers too. Because when he made her laugh it felt like a victory, and when they laughed together it felt like *life.* Because kissing her was his new favourite hobby. Because when she thought he needed something, she stepped in and went the whole way—diamond, dress, heels and all.

Because she named the goat Genevieve,

and worried about who would look after it while she was gone.

Because he didn't know her whole story yet, and he wanted to. He wanted to know her, understand her, more than anyone else on the planet.

Because he wanted to be part of her story for the rest of his life.

Oh, hell.

Because he was in love with her. In a way that he'd never felt before, even with Milli.

He didn't want Milli back. He never had.

He didn't want another fake relationship. He wanted the real thing.

With Daisy.

Except she was standing there telling him to go back to Milli because one fake relationship was just like another.

'Is everything between us fake for you?' Jay asked, his head still spinning from his realisations.

Daisy gave him a sly smile. 'Is that a question about my bedroom satisfaction levels? Don't worry, Jay. I'm not going to go giving interviews casting shade on your manly prowess. You know that side of things wasn't fake at all. But that's just lust. Passion. Friends with benefits, right?'

'Friends with benefits.'

'Sure! Well, not now you're back together with Milli. But we'll still be friends—just like Nico said. It's the best of both worlds, right?'

'And you can give up what we had that easily?' Because he wasn't sure he could.

More than that, he knew for certain now that he didn't want to.

She shrugged again. 'We always knew it wasn't going to last for long, right? Once the new album came out, or the tours were over, we'd be going our separate ways any-way. This just brings it forward a bit.'

'I just…' He couldn't find the words.

'What? You thought I was just going to fall in love with you, like all those scream-ing fans?' She shot him an amused look, and Jay felt it stab his heart. 'Come on, Jay, you know me better than that.'

'I thought I did.' He'd thought he'd seen a

new side to her, the last few weeks. A Daisy no one else got to see, or have, or hold.

But apparently that had all been fake too.

'I might be younger than you, but I think I learned the most important rule a lot sooner than you did,' she said contemplatively. 'Always know what the person you're with wants from you. Because they always want something. Kevin wants you to be a star—and make him a lot of money. Nico wants you to leave him enough of the groupies to keep him happy. Harry, bless him, just wants you to be happy—but he's better than most people.'

'And you? What do you want from me?'

'I wanted to escape the tour and write some songs, and pretending to date you let me do that,' she said simply. 'And you wanted me to hang on your arm to show Milli you'd moved on, even when you hadn't.'

'That was then,' Jay pressed. 'That was before…everything that's happened between us. I'm asking you, what do you want from me now?'

Daisy shook her head. 'We agreed upfront what we both wanted, Jay. There's no point trying to change it now, just because we had sex and you're feeling sentimental about it.'

How could she feel so little, when he felt so much?

But then, it had been exactly the same with Milli, hadn't it? He'd been struck down by her leaving, and she'd just been playing a game.

He'd fallen for it again, when he'd sworn to himself that he wouldn't. He'd thought he was too wise, too cynical to the way this industry worked to be fooled again. But he was the same idiot who'd thought he was in love with Milli Masters.

Except this time it was Daisy, and he knew that was going to hurt a thousand times more.

'You're right.' The words didn't even feel like his. He couldn't believe he was saying them.

'I am?' Daisy asked, eyebrow raised. 'I mean, I usually am, but about what in particular?'

'One fake relationship is as good as another. And if I have to pick I might as well go with the one that's best for my career, right?' Swallowing, he drank in the sight of her one last time, here, in this place that had meant so much to them.

'Right. Of course.' Daisy shrugged. 'Makes sense.'

'I'll get the guys to get their stuff together, we'll head to wherever Milli's staying so I can talk with her. Then I guess we'll see you back on tour.'

'Great. I'll see you there.'

He wanted to kiss her. Or shake her. Or fall to his knees and beg her to think about this. To open her heart to the possibility of more.

But he didn't.

He turned around, walked back into the house, and consigned Daisy Mulligan to the graveyard of his heart.

CHAPTER ELEVEN

DAISY COULDN'T BEAR to be there when they left, so she walked down the hill into the village, glad she'd changed out of Jay's shirt and her shorts while Milli had made her impassioned plea for his heart. Not only was it not suitable attire for going out in public, but it smelled of him. Warm and comforting and safe.

She couldn't be smelling his clothes for comfort when she'd just walked out of his life. Or, not, because she had to face him on tour again in a week's time. And before then, she had to get him comprehensively out of her system.

So, first rule: no smelling his clothes. If he even left any behind.

God, she hoped he didn't find that T-shirt of his she'd hidden under her pillow. Not

262 ITALIAN ESCAPE WITH HER FAKE FIANCÉ

that she was going to smell it, because that was breaking the rules and—

She sobbed, stopped walking, and sat down on the grass at the side of the road.

Okay. So it was possible she'd just made the biggest mistake of her life. But she'd done it to protect herself, the same as always. She was keeping her eye on the prize—chasing her dreams.

Except what was that dream worth without someone to share it with?

Pulling her phone from her pocket, she sent a group message to Aubrey and Jessica.

So, I might have done a stupid thing.

Aubrey responded almost instantly.

You? I don't believe it! Teasing! What's happened? Is it something to do with you getting engaged to Jay Barwell...?

It took surprisingly little time for Daisy to recount everything that had happened over the last couple of weeks to her friend, and by then Jessica had also jumped on the group chat.

Hmm... Are you sure he doesn't feel the same way about you?

Aubrey answered that.

Of course she's not sure! Because she never let on that she loved him! So how could he know?

Jessica came back:

Well, then. Maybe she should tell him.

Daisy shuddered at the thought of putting herself in that position—of opening her heart to Jay only to let him tear it apart.

If he felt the same he would have said, wouldn't he? I mean, he had the chance, when I told him that we'd agreed to a fake relationship. He could have said if he wanted something more, and he didn't.

Aubrey: But neither did you. And you obviously do.

Jessica: Aubrey's right.

Aubrey: I love it when you say that!

Jessica: He might be scared, like you.

Daisy: He's been voted world's sexiest man. Three times. How scared can he be?

Aubrey: That's not the same as love, and you know it.

Jessica: Plus his ex dumped him on social media before she came grovelling back. Trust might be an issue.

Daisy thought of Jay the night after the awards ceremony in Rome, telling her how he just wanted to demand Milli explain *why* she'd done it. She knew that feeling of not understanding something that had turned her life upside down.

She'd never been able to ask her mother

why she'd left, either. Nothing beyond her parting words about chasing her dreams.

She didn't even know if she'd ever found them.

That kind of uncertainty…yeah. That had an effect on a person.

But even if he did have non-fake feelings for me, he loved Milli. Of course he's going back to her if there's a chance of them being happy together.

Even though she was pretty certain it would only end the same way again.

Aubrey replied.

Then why did he ask you what to do?

Daisy bit her lip. As ever, her friend had a point. She'd been so busy protecting her own heart she hadn't even thought about his.

What if he'd wanted her to say, *Don't go back to Milli*?

She frowned. No. She wasn't going to

blame herself for this. If he wanted her he could have said as much too.

But if neither of them had the courage to try…

Jessica replied.

I guess the biggest question you have to ask yourself is…if you weren't afraid of anything, what would you want to do right now?

She didn't even have to think before answering.

I'd run back up the hill to the villa, to my home, and ask Jay to stay there with me. For real this time, not fake.

Then that's what you need to do. Run, girl! Or, trust me, you'll always regret it.

Could she?

Daisy shook her head. How could she not?

Jumping to her feet, she ran, only slowing as she crested the top of the hill and saw the driveway, empty except for a forlorn-looking Genevieve.

She didn't need to open the front door to know for sure; she could feel it already.

Jay had gone.

'You're being an idiot about this.' Harry, as ever, was perfectly happy being blunt about his brother's life choices, Jay realised.

'No. I'm focussing on what really matters. The band. The music,' he argued as he dumped his suitcase on yet another hotel bed. Just like all the other ones, except for one important fact. Somewhere in this hotel, according to Kevin's mysterious means of intelligence gathering, was Milli Masters. Probably the penthouse suite, if Jay had to guess.

He hated hotels, he'd decided. Even penthouse suites.

He missed the cottage already. He missed Daisy. He even missed the damn goat.

'I heard the song you and Daisy were working on when you played it for Kevin last night. She's better for the music than Milli could ever be.'

'I'm not disagreeing with you on that.' Jay pulled out a pair of tracksuit bottoms and searched for a T-shirt to wear with them. He was going to order room service, watch bad hotel TV, and slob about. That was his entire plan for the evening.

Milli and everything else could wait one more day. He couldn't take another emotional conversation today.

'Then why the hell are you running back to Milli Masters?' Harry grabbed the clothing from his hands to make Jay turn and look at him.

Jay wondered quite how stupid his brother thought he was. 'I didn't say I was going back to Milli.'

'That's what you told Daisy. And Kevin definitely thinks you are.'

'Firstly, you shouldn't be eavesdropping on my conversations. And secondly... Kevin believes what he wants to believe. But this time he's going to be disappointed. Now, can I have my clothes back, please?'

A calmness had settled over him as he'd walked away from Daisy. A certainty, one that made everything suddenly very simple.

He wasn't in love with Milli. Daisy wasn't in love with him.

And Jay didn't want a fake relationship with either of them.

He wanted the real thing. And if that meant waiting until his star had faded and no one was interested in dating him for his celebrity, that was fine by him.

Harry handed him his trousers. 'So... what are you doing?'

Jay changed out of the jeans he'd travelled in. 'I'm taking a leaf out of your book, Harry. I'm waiting for the real thing to come along. No more fake celebrity romances. The next time I get into a relationship it will be a real one. Now, where the hell are all my T-shirts?'

'You're waiting for a real relationship,' Harry said, disbelief colouring his voice.

'You don't think I can do it?'

'I think you're even more of an idiot than I thought.'

Jay stopped searching for a T-shirt and raised an eyebrow at his brother. 'Excuse me?'

'What do you think you had with Daisy?'

Everything I ever wanted.

Jay clenched his jaw and forced the thought aside. 'Exactly what we agreed we'd have. A fake relationship—fake engagement, even. And a friends-with-benefits arrangement. That's all.'

'Did she tell you that?'

'She didn't need to. It's what we agreed.' Except he couldn't remember actually agreeing to it. It just sort of happened. Like falling for her. He definitely hadn't planned to do that.

'She told you that,' Harry said smugly. 'Okay, Jay, think about what you know about Daisy.'

How she laughs. How she looks when she's sleeping. How she kisses. How she writes songs. How she feels in my arms...

'She's defensive, prickly, sarcastic and mocking is her favourite hobby,' he said instead.

'Exactly.' Harry beamed. 'Now, look at this.'

He pulled out his phone, but Jay pushed it away.

'I don't want to see any more photos of Daisy pretending she's in love with me for an audience.'

'That's not what this is,' Harry said. 'Just watch it. Please?'

Sighing, Jay took the phone and pressed play.

He recognised Daisy's cottage instantly, but not the angle. In the video, Daisy was sitting cross-legged in the armchair, her guitar in her lap, laughing at something he'd said.

'Play it for me again,' he heard his own voice say, and saw himself appear on the screen, perching on the coffee table opposite her, his own guitar in his hands. 'I want to try something.'

Daisy nodded, then started to play.

It was the second song they'd written together. The one that had led to the almost kiss that had led to everything that came after.

The moment he'd realised that she might want him too.

'Where did you get this?' he asked, hoarsely.

'Daisy sent it to me. She said she always records song-writing sessions on her phone in case she forgets something later. I asked her if she had any footage of the songs you were working on together and she sent me this.'

'And when you're close, oh, how I feel you. Down deep inside my soul,' Daisy sang on the screen.

Jay pressed stop.

He couldn't hear that right now.

He handed Harry the phone back, and his brother took it reluctantly.

'I'm sending you the file,' he said, tapping the screen. 'Watch it to the end, will you? Then tell me if you honestly think you still have to wait for the real thing. Because I'm telling you, if I had someone who looked at me the way Daisy looks at you—or the way you look at her—I'd be shouting it from the rooftop.'

'You're wrong,' Jay said. But somewhere inside, part of him was wondering. Hoping.

'No,' Harry said. 'I'm not. Watch the video. I'm going to go tell Kevin to stop planning your grand reunion with Milli.'

She didn't want to leave.

Daisy looked around her cosy villa, no longer crumbling quite so much, but still in need of some redecoration and sprucing up. Maybe she could just stay here. Cancel the tour—or, better yet, Kevin could probably get Milli Masters to fill in for her. Jay would like that.

Except Milli would expect to headline, of course.

And she didn't want to think about Milli and Jay.

She'd known, when she'd ended things with him, that she'd have to be back on that tour bus with him within the week. But she'd hoped the few days apart would help her get over that crushing sense of loss that had hit her when she'd returned to the villa to discover it was just her and Genevieve now.

They hadn't.

Jessica and Aubrey had been great, messaging every day to check in with her, trying to keep her spirits up. They'd both also tried to talk to her about the conversations she needed to have with Jay when she saw him again, but she'd managed to shut them down. She wasn't ready to think about that just yet.

She knew what she needed to do to get through the first couple of weeks back on tour with the band—the same thing she'd been doing since long before she left home at sixteen. Toughen up and not let anyone see she cared.

If the guys realised how she felt about Jay it would be awkward. If Milli realised, it would be humiliating. And if the world knew…she'd be a laughing stock.

'It's not like I'm the first girl who had a guy not love her back,' she said to Genevieve. 'I'll survive.'

The only thing was, when she'd been with Jay, for the first time in so long it hadn't felt like surviving.

It had felt like really living.

On the counter, her phone flashed with an alert, and she picked it up to find a message from Aubrey.

Did you see this?

Frowning, she clicked the link. Milli Masters' perfect face filled the screen— except she didn't look *quite* so perfect for once. There were artfully placed tears in the corners of her eyes, but Daisy suspected that was a filter, because if anything her expression looked more annoyed than upset.

She turned up the volume to hear the words, and her breath caught in her throat.

'I mean, when it comes down to it, I'm just another heartbroken girl. I thought we were soul mates, but I guess sometimes true love just doesn't work out, right? But I wish Jay every happiness, and I'd hate for any of you to give him a hard time.'

Daisy scoffed at that. Knowing Milli's fans the hate mail was probably already in full swing.

But she'd worry about that later. Right now, she needed to understand what this meant.

'Does it mean he hasn't gone back to her after all?' she asked aloud.

Genevieve remained unhelpfully silent, busy chewing on the fringe of an old sofa cushion.

'Or does it mean…?'

'It means I'm in love with someone else. And I'm hoping she's in love with me too.'

Daisy spun around at the sound of Jay's voice, half expecting it to be her imagination tormenting her. But no, there he was, standing in the open doorway, the Italian sun streaming through his light hair, his hands in his pockets as he squinted at her.

'Are you wearing my T-shirt?'

'Are you really here?' she countered. She wasn't about to confess now that she'd been wearing one of the three T-shirts he'd managed to leave behind every day for the last week.

'Yeah. I figured I left some stuff behind here.'

'Like your T-shirts?'

'And my heart.'

'Oh.' Her own heart was hammering against her chest, a constant reminder that it was still inside her and beating and loving and that maybe she might consider just *listening* to it for once.

And for the first time since she couldn't remember when—Daisy decided to do just that.

This would be so much easier if she didn't look like a startled rabbit. An adorable startled rabbit wearing his T-shirt, but still. Her eyes—wide and confused—were giving nothing away. He'd been so sure—well, Harry had been sure enough for both of them—that if he came back then they could figure it all out. Even Kevin had thought it was a good idea—if only because, if Milli wasn't in Jay's future, he wanted to make sure that they at least had Daisy back on tour, along with the new songs they had written.

But now he was here, looking into those wide eyes, other than the relief of being with her again, Jay wasn't sure of anything at all.

No. That wasn't true. He was sure of one thing: he couldn't risk not trying.

He'd called his mum, in the end. Asked her to tell him all about his dad, about their relationship. How she knew it was the for ever kind of love.

'Honestly, Jay?' his mum had said. *'I'm not sure you can ever know for sure— maybe not until it's gone. But you can hope. You can take a chance and you can work for it, if she's worth it. Because if it is* true *love, then it'll all work out. If it doesn't it wasn't meant to be. You can't know which it is without trying, and without hope and hard work.'*

So Jay took a step closer, and hoped.

'I came back because I realised I was wrong. One fake relationship wasn't anything like the other. When I was with Milli... I thought our relationship was something that it wasn't. I believed that we could have a future together. That we could love each other. And when I realised that she'd never believed either of those things... it shook my faith in love altogether.'

'I know,' Daisy said quietly, but there was still a hint of her old mocking tones in her voice that made him smile. 'You were grumpy as anything when we started this tour together.'

'But you changed that.'

'That much sex will cheer anyone up,' she joked.

Jay shook his head. 'You just can't stop yourself, can you? I meant the faith-in-love thing, not just the being grumpy.'

'Oh.' That, at least, seemed to render her speechless. Jay decided he'd better get in with what else he needed to say before she found another flip remark to make.

'Because the thing is, Daisy, being in a fake relationship with you felt more real than any real relationship I've ever had.

And I think we gave up on it too quick, because we were both scared of getting it wrong. At least, I know I was. You were so adamant that it was all for show that I believed you, even though I knew for me it was something more. And maybe you don't feel the same—maybe it really was just all fake for you. And if that's the case, I'll get over it, eventually, I'm sure. But if you *do*—if you think there might be something real between us underneath all the pretending…well, I'd never forgive myself if I didn't find out.'

He stopped and waited for her response. It didn't come.

Doubt started to creep into Jay's mind. Maybe her jokes were attempts at deflection—to avoid having this conversation in the first place. To stop him making a fool of himself because, despite everything, Daisy wasn't cruel.

Maybe Harry was wrong.

He felt a rough lapping at his hand and looked down to find Genevieve nibbling on his fingers. At least someone seemed genuinely pleased to see him, if only because she was hoping he'd brought food.

But Daisy was still staring at him.

'I'm sorry,' he said. 'Maybe I—'

'No!' Lurching forward, Daisy grabbed his hand and held it against her T-shirt-clad chest. 'No. I'm sorry. I... I lied when I said it was all fake. I lied because I was scared. Because I'd just figured out that I was in love with you, and you were going back to Milli—'

'I never went back to Milli. Not for one night.'

She shook her head. 'It doesn't matter. The point is, I was terrified of getting my heart broken. Of feeling more for you than I knew what to do with and not wanting anything in return. And if you didn't want me as a fake fiancée, I didn't know what you wanted from me at all, and that scared me. In my world...you always need to know what the deal is. What you're giving and what you're getting. Or what you're giving up.'

'I would never ask you to give up anything,' he swore.

She flashed him a small smile and carried on. 'And with you… I just felt so much, *got* so much. And I didn't know what you wanted in return.'

'You,' he whispered. 'All you ever have to be for me is yourself. Because just being with you gives me everything I need. Music, laughter, passion—and love. Those are all I want in this world. Well, those and truth.'

'I could give you those,' Daisy whispered, and when she looked up at him there was such hope in her eyes that Jay knew that, from now on, everything would be all right. As long as they were together.

Reaching into his pocket, he pulled out a small box. 'Harry gave me this to give to you.' He flipped it open. 'It's our grandma's engagement ring. Seems he knew how I felt about you before even I did, when he asked mum for it.'

'It's beautiful.' Daisy seemed mesmerised by the twisting lines of silver, specked with tiny diamonds and sapphires.

'It's nothing like as valuable as the one I bought you in Rome, but—'

'But it's *real*.'

'I was going to say you can play guitar wearing it.'

She grinned at that. 'That too. But, Jay—'

'The whole world already thinks we're engaged. And I don't want to rush you into anything—we can wait years to get married if that's what you need. But I'd like you to wear this ring. So whenever I'm not there to remind you, you'll know that I love you.'

Wordlessly, she held up her left hand and Jay slipped the huge diamond from her finger and replaced it with his grandmother's ring, love and happiness pulsing through every inch of him. 'Marry me, Daisy? For real?'

'For real,' she agreed, reaching up to kiss him. 'And for always.'

EPILOGUE

WELL, I HAVE to confess that's not exactly how I expected things to go.

I didn't need the report that landed on my desk that morning to follow the effects of *this* gift. Max and I had watched the whole thing play out in real time on social media, with Max begging for snacks at my side and me handing them over because I was so distracted by the twists and turns of the story.

One thing I didn't know, however—and possibly never will—was how much of what I saw was real and how much fabricated for the media. Maybe Daisy will tell me one day if I ask.

She hasn't contacted me yet, but I suspect she will soon. She'll have questions, I'm sure.

I spotted her through the crowds that

night in Rome, but resisted the urge to seek her out. When one is giving a person something they *need*, sometimes it's better to stay out of the way until *they* realise that they need it too. At least in my experience.

When I saw Milli Masters, of all people, standing in front of the old cottage where I used to holiday as a child, I was worried that the whole plan might have backfired horribly. The romance part was outside my control, of course—all I did was give Daisy a place to escape, a place to call her own. Who she took there with her was entirely her own choice.

But I hated to think that the place might become associated with such bad memories that she'd shut it up and never go back there. Max and I definitely had a few sleepless nights over that one.

Then, this morning, when I knew that Daisy must already be back on tour with her beau and his band, she posted a photo on social media. Her and Jay and a goat, standing on a cliff, with the cottage in the background. He had one arm around her waist, the other presumably holding the camera, and she was on tiptoe kissing his cheek. The goat was eating his shirt, but he didn't seem to have noticed.

The caption underneath? One word: *Home*.

And that was when I knew that my gift had steered me right once again. I've given Daisy what she needed most in the world: a place of her own, where she can just be herself and know that's more than enough.

I just hope I can have the same success with Aubrey's gift...

* * * * *

LET'S TALK

Romance

For exclusive extracts, competitions
and special offers, find us online:

f facebook.com/millsandboon

⃝ @millsandboonuk

🐦 @millsandboon

Or get in touch on 0844 844 1351*

For all the latest titles coming soon,
visit millsandboon.co.uk/nextmonth